Critical Acclaim for

IT WASN'T ME

A *Publishers Weekly* Best Book of the Year

A Winter Kids' Indie Next List Selection

A Junior Library Guild Selection

An Amazon Spotlight Pick of the Month

A Massachusetts Book Awards Honor Book

An ILA Children's Choice

★ "What at first seems like a novel solely about bullying becomes a story about six kids who find their way to **true friendship and fierce loyalty**, and why restorative justice is worth the time and effort it takes."
—*Publishers Weekly*, starred review

★ "A timely, introspective whodunit with **a lot of heart**."
—*Kirkus Reviews*, starred review

★ "Levy writes in an easy style with **laugh-out-loud humor**, offering characters that slowly reveal **deeper complexity**."
—*School Library Journal*, starred review

IT WASN'T ME

Also by Dana Alison Levy

The Misadventures of the Family Fletcher

The Family Fletcher Takes Rock Island

This Would Make a Good Story Someday

IT WASN'T ME

Dana Alison Levy

A Yearling Book

This is a work of fiction. Names, characters, places, and incidents either are the product of the author's imagination or are used fictitiously. Any resemblance to actual persons, living or dead, events, or locales is entirely coincidental.

Text copyright © 2018 by Dana Alison Levy
Cover art copyright © 2018 by Bobby McKenna

All rights reserved. Published in the United States by Yearling, an imprint of Random House Children's Books, a division of Penguin Random House LLC, New York. Originally published in hardcover in the United States by Delacorte Press, an imprint of Random House Children's Books, New York, in 2018.

Yearling and the jumping horse design are registered trademarks of Penguin Random House LLC.

Visit us on the Web! rhcbooks.com

Educators and librarians, for a variety of teaching tools, visit us at RHTeachersLibrarians.com

Library of Congress Cataloging-in-Publication Data is available upon request.

ISBN 978-1-5247-6646-7 (paperback)

Printed in the United States of America
10 9 8 7 6 5 4 3 2 1
First Yearling Edition 2020

To the teachers and educators who do the
hard work of helping our kids find their way.
And especially to the ones in my family:
Steve, Mary, Tracey, Pat, Paul, Peggy, Erica,
and Gen . . . Ms. Lewistons, all.

CHAPTER 1

Day One Assessments

SHIPTON MIDDLE SCHOOL

*Please fill out the following questions as honestly
and completely as you can. There are no wrong answers.*

Date: Feb. 18

Name: *Molly Claremont*

**What happened and what were you thinking at the
time of the incident?**

*I have LITERALLY NO IDEA. I was waiting to be
picked up and I wandered into the student gallery,
which isn't a crime, last I checked. And the photos
were totally ruined, which was really surprising and,*

you know, upsetting. Because of course our school is no place for vandalism and bullying.

But I just walked in there. And the next day, when someone opened the darkroom door and ruined Theo's stuff again? That was horrible, and I feel so bad for him. Our community definitely needs to come together and make this a Bully-Free Zone. I should bring it up with student council. Maybe we can do a bake sale for Theo. Anyway, I realize I don't have an alibi, but why would I touch his stuff?

I can't see how it has anything to do with me.

What have you thought about since?
Well, to be totally honest (because we're supposed to be honest here, right?), I'm mostly thinking how RIDICULOUS it is that I'm being blamed for ruining Theo's photos. I'm sure it feels terrible for him, having his work destroyed like that, with people writing such horrible, embarrassing stuff. The whole school can't stop talking about it. But still. It's NOT MY FAULT.

What about this has been hardest for you?
Again, if I'm being honest, I CANNOT BELIEVE I HAVE TO SPEND AN ENTIRE WEEK HERE IN THIS DETENTION ROOM (or Justice Circle room,

or whatever). I get that this is a big deal, but it wasn't me.

What do you think needs to be done to make things as right as possible?

We'll obviously need to establish a better Say No to Bullying campaign. I'll definitely be bringing it up with the student council. We don't want vandals and criminals in the school. But it has nothing to do with me. NOTHING.

Is there anything at all you'd like to share confidentially with Ms. Lewiston?

No.

Name: Andre Hall

What happened and what were you thinking at the time of the incident?

I dropped my bag off in the student gallery and went to the bathroom before going home. I didn't want to bring my bag in with me because that bathroom floor is nasty. So I left my bag, then on the way back realized I had forgotten my lab notebook. It was fifteen minutes before I got back to the gallery, and by then Theo's photos were totally ruined. Whoever it was, they weren't playing. It was bad. But like I keep saying, I wasn't even there. When I walked back to get my bag, there were a ton of people in the gallery, all freaking out.

What have you thought about since?

It was pretty intense. I've never seen anything like it at our school before. I mean, that was some severe destruction. And some rude stuff written on the photos of Theo. I'd want to transfer schools if that happened to me. And then the very next day someone messed with his stuff in the darkroom? It seems like someone's got it in for him.

But I don't know ... does he have enemies or something? I barely know the guy. It's not like he talks to me. And like I keep saying, I wasn't even there until after.

What about this has been hardest for you?

It's a bummer that no one even noticed that I wasn't there, and that it was only my bag sitting on the bench. Though maybe whoever did it figured it would be better to have more suspects or something. I was planning on spending vacation week practicing a ton with my band, and now I'm stuck here. And since my bandmates go to a different school, it's hard to get rehearsal time. We have some big stuff coming up, and we were counting on this week. But it's obviously worse for Theo. I mean, he must be freaking out. I know I would be.

What do you think needs to be done to make things as right as possible?

I guess catch the guy who did it and make him apologize? Not really sure since I didn't have anything to do with it.

Is there anything at all you'd like to share confidentially with Ms. Lewiston?

Just ... how could nobody notice that I wasn't there?

Name: *Erik Estrale*

What happened and what were you thinking at the time of the incident?

I don't really remember. I had a huge game against Greenfield that night, and I was mostly thinking about whether I'd be starting point guard. (I was. I scored 19 points. It was a totally sick game. Coach gave me the Golden Jockstrap.)

What have you thought about since?

I don't know. I didn't do it, so I just want to get out of here.

What about this has been hardest for you?

I was supposed to do a full-day basketball camp this week with the whole team, and Coach was seriously mad when he heard I can't make it. He said I shouldn't expect to start if I get in trouble at school.

What do you think needs to be done to make things as right as possible?

I don't know. I mean, I figure Theo must have made someone really mad. Like, is he in a fight with anyone? I feel really sorry for the guy. But I don't know what to do for him.

Is there anything at all you'd like to share confidentially with Ms. Lewiston?
What happens if no one confesses at the end of this whole thing? Will it all go away?

Name: Alice Shu

What happened and what were you thinking at the time of the incident?
Actually, I remember EXACTLY what I was thinking, because I was trying to figure out if it would be possible to do a knife wound on a zombie, or if, since there's no blood, there's not much point. (This is special effects for my movies, obvs.) Anyway, I had been pondering this and I walked into the wall by the water fountain near the student gallery and smacked my shoulder hard enough to drop my books. By the time I picked everything up I had missed the bus. I had to wait for a ride and I knew it would be a while, so I decided to walk over to the gallery. When I got there Molly Claremont was FREAKING OUT. I've never seen anyone turn that color red. Maybe she

had never read any of those words before ... they were pretty bad. Poor Theo. Then the very next day his stuff was ruined again in the darkroom! Someone must be out to get him. Maybe there's a secret stalker. Maybe that person is in this room right now....

What have you thought about since?

Zombies look dumb with knives sticking out of them. Without blood, or at least a festering wound, there's really nothing happening, and since they're undead, it just sticks out looking stupid. OH! You mean Theo's photos? Well, I guess someone really hates him. Or the idea of him. A lot of people say they can't stand me but they don't even know me. They just assume.

What about this has been hardest for you?

I don't really care. I didn't have plans this week, other than working on some special effects. But I can do them after detention. Or Justice Circle, or whatever we're calling this.

What do you think needs to be done to make things as right as possible?

Well, it'd be great if there was a huge zombie revenge scene, where Theo is commanding the undead to get back at whoever trashed his stuff. But in real life, there's not much we can do when jerks mess with us. I'm sure Theo's really embarrassed, but he shouldn't worry. It will all die down and people will forget about it. I would know.

Is there anything at all you'd like to share confidentially with Ms. Lewiston?

Do you really think people will tell the truth here?

Name: Jax Fletcher

What happened and what were you thinking at the time of the incident?

Nothing. I don't remember anything about that day. It was another ~~stupid~~ school day.

What have you thought about since?

No one knows who did it, so I don't really know why we have to be here. Without proof isn't this against the law or something? My parents okayed it because they're always down for some new age talk-it-out-and-everyone-will-feel-better stuff. But give me a break.

What about this has been hardest for you?

I'll probably get in more trouble for saying this, but I HATE SCHOOL. And now I have to spend vacation week here.

What do you think needs to be done to make things as right as possible?

Theo needs to get over it. There's no point in this.

Is there anything at all you'd like to share confidentially with Ms. Lewiston?

What do we have to do to get out of here???????

CHAPTER 2

Let Us Consider Gnawing Off Our Limbs and Escaping

I remember ages ago reading about how some animals, if caught in a trap, will gnaw off the captured limb to attempt to escape. It stuck with me, because (1) it's sort of awesome yet disgusting to imagine actually *chewing off your own paw*, and (2) I wondered if the animal would just die after, what with blood loss and infection and the fact it would now be totally slow and easy dinner for any predator hanging around. Is that *really* a good survival strategy? I'm skeptical.

But I think now I get why the animal might take a chance.

I'm trying to maintain some chill, but since the biggest, most dramatic act of vandalism in our school's history happened to my photos and *I'm* spending vacation week at school, it seems like the kind of scenario where one might be compelled to gnaw off a limb and try to escape, bleeding and limping out the door.

My mom said I didn't have to do this. That it was understandable if I was traumatized by it and needed time away from school to process. But I'm not traumatized. I refuse to be traumatized. That would imply that I care what these losers think about my photographs. I mean, yes, it was horrifying and embarrassing to have the entire school talking about what happened, whispering and pointing and repeating the garbage someone wrote all over the pictures. But I need to move on. None of these people will grow up to be art critics, I'm sure. The only thing I find traumatic is the amount of Axe body spray in this classroom.

As of right now, I have the five tweenbots who might have done it staring everywhere in the room but at me, like my face is some kind of anti-magnet to their eyes.

But Ms. Lewiston isn't having it.

"Please move your chairs. Remember, this is a Justice *Circle*. Not a Justice Line, or a Justice Blob." She smiles, but no one smiles back.

Poor Ms. Lewiston. It's going to be a long week.

People shuffle their chairs around, and like one of those "Which Time Lord Are You?" *Doctor Who* quizzes online, I swear I can tell everything about these clowns by the way they get into position.

First: Molly Claremont, Overachiever Extraordinaire, hops up like she sat on a tack and moves her chair so that it's directly opposite mine. Great. I'm now all deer-in-the-headlights with her staring right at me. I preferred the anti-magnet thing.

Second: Next to her, Andre Hall gets up and repositions his chair by lifting it and putting it back down so that it doesn't make a sound. I barely even saw him move; he just went from one spot to another. I doubt anyone noticed him, kind of like how he gets through school.

Third: Erik Estrale lifts his chair too, but one-handed, bringing it up and down a few times like he's doing reps with a weight, then lets it drop with a clatter. *Then,* when he finally sits, he immediately gets up, cracks his neck a few times, and sits back down. Dude is such a jockstrap.

Fourth: Jax Fletcher, of course, drags his chair across the floor, making it scrape as loud as possible, which makes Molly put her hands over her ears and shriek. For the record, it wasn't *that* loud. Then Jax flips the chair backward, straddles it, and hangs his arms over the back. He taptap-taps his foot like he can't wait to get out of here. Get comfortable, buddy. We have six more hours before any of us go anywhere.

Fifth: Ms. Lewiston is trying to be patient, I think, but if I were taking bets, I'd put money on her losing it with Alice

Shu, the last of our little club, before the week is up. Alice isn't like Jax, who's basically a black belt at bugging people until they lose it. But she's So. Freaking. Out of it. Like now, while we're supposed to be getting into this circle, she's sitting as far away as possible, staring out the window and whispering to herself. Also it should be noted that she has a massive and nasty-looking black eye.

"Alice? Can you join us?" Ms. Lewiston asks, her voice still bright. "And do you want me to get some ice for that eye?"

Alice jumps like a cat—literally twitches all over—then, looking confused, gets up and starts dragging her chair forward. Of course the strap of her Sharpie-doodled messenger bag is stuck under the chair leg, so she has to stop and untangle it. Then her bag spills, so she carefully picks up all the pens, index cards, gum wrappers, notebooks, and pencil cases (she has, like, six different pencil cases). For five minutes we all silently watch her get her stuff together. Finally she sits down between Molly and Andre. Molly, being Molly, makes her patented Everything Smells Awful face and moves closer to Erik.

"Ice, hon?" Ms. Lewiston asks again.

Alice looks, if possible, even more confused. Maybe she's sleepwalking. . . . She doesn't seem to grasp even the basic idea of what's happening.

"Why would I need ice?" she asks, and her voice is high and clear, like she should be singing or something.

"Your eye . . . ," Ms. Lewiston starts, and Alice starts laughing. We all keep staring while she slaps her knee, which I didn't realize was something people actually did outside of books. Finally she snorts a few times and shakes her head.

"This is makeup! Sorry. I didn't mean to freak you out," she says finally, collecting herself.

Molly can't quite take this. "You did that to yourself on *purpose*?" she asks, squinting at Alice.

Alice nods so hard she looks like a bobblehead doll. "Of course! Special-effects makeup. You know, horror films, slasher movies, all that stuff?"

Molly visibly recoils, and, for extra fun, turns white, then red. "Ohmygod. Like, literally, you could not be weirder if you tried."

Alice blinks. "What if I had *two* black eyes? That would be weirder, right?"

"Oh. My. God!" Molly leans back.

Alice leans forward. She peers right at Molly. "I could do *such* sick bruising on you. You're so pale, and the freckles would be really fun to work with."

Erik snickers, then tries to cover it as a cough. Alice turns around.

"And you too!" she says, looking far more awake now. "I think we could do something *spectacular* with a compound fracture for you. You know, bone poking out through the skin? Epic."

Erik immediately freezes, prey-like. Now I'm the one trying to make my laugh sound like a cough. This is actually more entertaining than I expected.

But Ms. Lewiston isn't going to let us wander down the road to Aliceland. She takes a deep breath, then lets it out. "Special effects! That is really cool. You'll have to tell us more about that at some point. But right now, I'm going to ask us all to redirect our attention to this circle, and to the reason we're here. Okay?"

Silence.

She looks around the circle, making eye contact with each of us. *"Okay?"* she says again, and this time we all stare at our laps and make that muttering *yesweagreejustleave-usalone* noise that keeps most teachers happy.

But Ms. Lewiston isn't most teachers.

She's silent long enough that we all look at her. I will tell you: there is no one tough enough not to squirm a little at the expression on her face.

"Listen," she says, and takes another deep breath. "There's no point in being here."

I lean back. *Finally.* Someone agrees with me. Maybe I won't have to gnaw off my own leg to get out of here. But she goes on.

"There's no point in being here *if* we don't do the work. If you're all going to sit here, trying to be as tough and silent as possible—"

Alice interrupts. "Oh, I don't need to be tough and silent," she says, again in her singsong voice. "I'd much rather talk."

Ms. Lewiston smiles at her, and, who knows how, but it looks like a real smile. "Thanks, Alice. But I'm going to need *everyone* to talk, and no matter how hard or awkward it is, we're going to have to talk about what happened with Theo's photographs."

Like magic, twelve eyes swivel to point at me. Mentally, channeling my inner trapped wolf, I start to gnaw at my leg.

Compared with this detention, a little pain and blood loss seem like reasonable options.

Sorry, not detention. *Justice Circle,* which sounds like we should light candles and do that weird *ommmmm* breathing my mom does in yoga. But no, we're in a room with fluorescent lights, two-tone brown tile floor, and the unmistakable smell of that baked ziti/chicken patty/pizza mix. I swear the whole school smells like those three foods, even if the cafeteria hasn't served them in weeks.

Who knows why? Who knows why anything happens in this place? Certainly not me. And if we're going to point the stern finger of blame for this whole thing, it should go right . . . to . . . Ms. Lewiston.

This was her idea. Instead of suspending the five suspected students who were found on the scene after the epically scaled total public destruction of my photographs, she thought we should all sit down over vacation week and *talk about it*. Our principal, Ms. Davis, was not at all convinced. I was waiting outside the office while the two of them were going at it, and let's just say I don't know who Ms. Davis likes less, Ms. Lewiston or students. Might be a tie.

Imagine those massive male moose bellowing and charging at each other like you'd see on National Geographic. It was nothing like that physically. Because it was two middle-aged women talking politely to each other. But *mentally,* it totally was.

Ms. Davis: Zero tolerance has to mean ZERO TOLERANCE. That's what it means. ZERO TOLERANCE.

Ms. Lewiston: . . .

Ms. Davis: Well? Do you not agree?

Ms. Lewiston: Sorry, I didn't realize that was a question. I agree that vandalism and bullying

shouldn't be tolerated. But suspending five
students who have not been proven guilty of
anything seems . . . problematic.

Ms. Davis: Well, I still—

Ms. Lewiston: And I can't help but think the
school committee will be very upset.

Ms. Davis: . . .

Mentioning the school committee was a total Jedi move. Ms. Davis looked like she had just vomited in her mouth, but she listened while Ms. Lewiston outlined the whole Justice Circle idea, and finally gave a rather ungracious and terse agreement. And I guess the parents all agreed because it seemed like the best option: while no one was being formally charged with a crime yet, these five were the only ones standing in the gallery after the vandalism was discovered. And somehow no one had managed a very convincing story about some masked stranger who snuck in and scribbled threats, gay slurs, and other misery all over my photographs before slipping out a window undetected. I overheard Davis saying that the kids only agreed because their parents hope they can get away with this Justice Circle instead of a hate crime on their record. And while I'd love to think they're here because they care so deeply about me, I suspect that for once she's right.

So yeah. Instead of the five of them getting suspended, we'll spend vacation week here, getting our justice on. Ms. Lewiston wrote a letter and told us all about this Justice Circle, that what she's trying to do is like a process schools and even courts use to help resolve disputes. It's partly based on Native American tribal models of justice, which are less about punishment and more about repairing the community.

We watched a video of a guy giving a TED Talk on it. I didn't know what a TED Talk was (and I learned it has *nothing* to do with a guy named Ted), but it's cool—seriously, like these criminals and drunk drivers and their victims sit in a circle with a therapist and deal with this really heavy stuff, being totally honest and deep. And (in the video, at least) everyone is way better off afterward. Like, the victims have closure and a feeling of peace, and these gang members or whatever work to make amends and then hopefully go on to be productive members of society. All cool.

But . . . please.

I agreed to do this, which I totally didn't have to do, for a few key reasons:

1) Because, not to sound completely sad (cue the tiny violin), I didn't really have plans for vacation anyway.

2) I have a pretty good idea how it went down and who in this room might have done it. But I have no proof, obviously, and who knows? Maybe Weird Alice or Silent Andre have their own reasons for ruining my stuff. Heck, maybe Molly had a freak-out of epic proportions and did something less than totally perfect for the first time in her life. I have no clue. But let's just say that spending a week here and avoiding having the person who did this get suspended, then hating on me for the rest of his natural-born life . . . well, five days doesn't seem like too big a price to pay not to be the seventh-grade equivalent of chum in the shark-infested water.

3) And finally, because Ms. Lewiston is one of the few non-horrible teachers in the school. Her non-horribleness was critical last year, when my dad left and I was kind of messed up. She'd let me sit in her office and chill and maybe talk books or photography until I didn't feel like crawling into a hole to die. So I owe her. After all, this Justice Circle is Ms. Lewiston's passion. And she's cool enough that I want to help out.

So here we are, sitting in a circle with Ms. Lewiston, while Ms. Davis—who made it clear she would rather be on vacation—prowls in and out of the room, staring ominously at different kids (okay, mostly Jax and Alice—Jax because he gets in trouble a lot, and Alice because she's, well . . . *Alice*) and reminding us—as if we needed reminding—that this isn't supposed to be fun. That we need to *make progress on the issue.*

But let's be real. We're a bunch of seventh graders at Shipton Middle School in small-town Massachusetts. The five kids in here besides me are the ones who were in the gallery right after it happened. They all swear they did nothing and know nothing and saw nothing. Andre swears he wasn't even there, that he had left his bag there and gone to the bathroom, but no one backed up his story. He's one of those kids who seriously blends into the background, so he may be telling the truth. And like I said, I'm pretty sure I know who gets the Most Likely to Vandalize Stuff Award.

So, sure, maybe we'll get a confession from Suspect Number One, or maybe someone else will actually speak up (Because really? No one saw *anything*? Please.) and drop some truth bombs. Or maybe no one will speak up and we'll end up right where we started. But . . . come on. It's not like this is a real crime. And it's not like anyone's going to suddenly be all "I CONFESS!" and admit it and "restore justice" to me.

I know who I'm dealing with. These are the same people I've been in school with since kindergarten. The Overachiever, the Jock, the Nerd, the Weirdo, and the Screwup. They all have their place in the school food chain, just like I do. And—honesty time—nothing that happens in this classroom is going to make a difference.

CHAPTER 3

Not to Be a Jerk, but
I Did My Part by Showing Up, Right?

Ms. Lewiston has us all ready to jump into this process, if by "jump into" you mean "do everything in our power to avoid eye contact." It's not pretty.

But she's got us in a circle, around a battery-powered candle on a piece of woven fabric that reminds me of the Guatemalan wall hanging my dad used to have in his office. Next to the fake candle, there's a bunch of smooth beach stones, a birch stick, and one those of shaky-eggs we used to play in kindergarten music class.

This does not look promising.

I try to remember why I'm here, but my reasons seem weaker than they did before. Somehow, being confronted with shaky-eggs and ceremonial rocks will do that to a dude.

"Remember," Ms. Lewiston says, looking at each of us.

"The goal here is not to punish or blame. It's to *understand and move forward*. Whoever did this to Theo has to be given a chance to see the impact of that damage. And Theo needs to be given a chance to share his hurt."

It takes military-school levels of self-control, but I do NOT roll my eyes in disgust. I'm pretty proud of myself for that, but apparently there are no rewards in this world, because Ms. Lewiston fixes on me.

"Look, Theo, you've been very strong about this, but I'm going to ask you to open up a bit, and talk about how these incidents have made you feel."

I let my hair fall in front of my face and stare at the desk. Uh-uh. Nope. I am not going to be the sacrificial lamb in this process.

Ms. Lewiston sighs. "Okay. Let's start with this. Why do you think it matters? Let's go around the circle. Jax? Do you want to start with the talking stick?"

Jax jerks in his seat and looks panicked. I'd feel bad for him if I wasn't so relieved that Lewiston found another target.

"Uhhhh . . . yeah. Sure." He leans down and picks up the birch stick. "So . . ." He pauses. "Wait. Can you remind me what we're supposed to do?"

Molly sighs in a loud Everyone Is a Moron way and says, "Don't you even *listen*? We're supposed to go around and say why you think it matters that we're here." She huffs and shifts in her seat, like Jax is personally offending her.

Ms. Lewiston coughs gently. "You're partly right, Molly, but remember, Jax has the talking stick. And this is a place of no judgment. Let's try to keep that in mind."

I try to turn my give-me-a-break laugh into a cough. No judgment is, I think, literally impossible for Molly Claremont.

But Jax is trying again, so we all dutifully give him our attention. "Well, uh . . . I guess it matters because Theo's photos were messed with, and you figure it's one of us, because we were the ones on the scene when it was discovered. Right?"

Ms. Lewiston nods. "Right. But why does that matter? Why does it matter to *you*?"

Jax scowls a little. "Truth? Because if no one gets caught, we're all basically guilty until proven innocent."

Andre shifts a little in his seat. Ms. Lewiston looks at him. "Thanks, Jax. Can you hand the stick to Andre now?"

Andre leans forward and takes it with the tips of his fingers, like it might be hot. "Well, I guess I think it matters because Theo's probably pretty upset. And he deserves to know who did it. And . . ." He pauses.

"Please go on, Andre," Ms. Lewiston says.

"Well, it's kind of harsh that Jax only cares about not

being in trouble. I mean, it's not really about us, right?" Andre carefully puts the stick down and leans back in his chair.

Ms. Lewiston looks around. "Anyone want to respond to that?"

Molly grabs the stick. "I don't think it's only about Theo. I mean, it's horrible about his photos, and I feel really sorry for him, but I don't think it's fair at all that I'm blamed for it."

"No one is blaming you, Molly," Ms. Lewiston says gently. "We're just trying to get to a better understanding of what happened."

Alice squeaks, then raises her hand. Molly hands over the stick. "If I say right now that I did it, that I trashed everything in the gallery and opened the darkroom door, would we all get to go home?"

Everyone tenses. I stare at her. Alice? Weird loner Alice was the one who did it? My pits get kind of sweaty, and I wrap my arms around myself. Seriously? I try to think of why she'd have it in for me, then give up, figuring it must have been some bizarro creepy goth thing. Maybe voices in her head told her to. But before I can follow this thread, she squeaks again.

"I mean, I didn't do it. *Obviously*. But I'm curious. Is that what the goal is? For someone to confess?"

We all lean back in our chairs. Talk about an anticlimax.

Erik clears his throat, then reaches for the stick, and I have to force myself not to flinch. I wonder what he'll say, because I'm pretty close to 100 percent certain he's Most Likely to Trash My Stuff, and he's big enough to do some serious damage with that stick. His camouflage Under Armour hoodie has to be size XXL, and I swear he probably has to shave already. Erik has never been leader of the geek bashing and wedgie giving, like his teammates, but as my grandfather used to say, "You can judge someone by the company they keep." And Erik keeps the company of the über jocks who spend many of their waking hours being total tormenting turds to the rest of us. And while I've never actually *seen* him doing anything, he's never stood up to his friends either. So yeah, my working hypothesis is that he's absolutely as much of a knuckle-dragging Neanderthal as they are. My basic strategy is classic prey: stay hidden, off the radar. Truth? Being in this Justice Circle with him makes me seriously nervous. I have to assume he's not so stupid that he'll try something in front of Ms. Lewiston, but still. Even having his big, mouth-breathing self looking at me feels downright dangerous.

When he gets the stick, he tosses it hand to hand like he's physically incapable of chilling out. "So, um. I just wanted to say that, well, based on that TED Talk about restorative justice, the point isn't really to punish us, but for us to figure out a way to understand what happened and make it up to Theo. And—" He pauses.

We're all watching Alice. She has taken out a ball of black yarn and a massive hook-shaped thing and is starting to do something crafty. She doesn't look up until Erik stops talking. Then she peers around at us and glares at him.

"WHAT?" she says loudly. Erik jumps a little.

"Well, just that it's not about punishment or finding someone guilty, but about understanding and moving forward."

I can't contain my eye roll. Apparently, Erik has swallowed the Justice Circle whole and is regurgitating it back up for Ms. Lewiston. He's now staring at his sneakers, but the tips of his ears are red. I wouldn't have thought Erik smart enough to do the double-fake ... to seem all into this whole justice thing so as not to make it glaringly obvious that he's the likeliest candidate for evil jock-overlord behavior. But what do I know? The world is a mysterious place.

Ms. Lewiston smiles like someone gave her a present. "That's exactly right, Erik. Thank you. Like Jax's and Molly's comments showed, it is about how someone's action affects all of us. And like Andre said, it's about re-alizing that Theo's been hurt, and it's only right that, as a community, we make it better."

Ms. Lewiston keeps talking, about the circle and our agreement to make this a safe space (whatever) and to respect the talking stick (sure) and to keep an open mind (doubtful). She's already explained most of this, so I tune out, staring around the room at the art projects that line the windowsill, the pile of books on the back desks (looks like they got to read *The Crossover,* which is freaking awesome despite being about basketball), and the flat gray winter light coming through the windows. It's ugly, but even so, I find pockets of interest, random stuff in shadow or the detailed mosaic on some kid's mosque diorama. Too bad I don't have my camera.

I make myself turn back to the circle. From the glazed eyes around me, I have to assume I'm not the only one zon-ing out. Glancing around at my fellow Justice Warriors, I am not optimistic that there's any deep thinking happen-ing. I wonder if anyone else is debating gnawing off a limb. Probably not . . . they're not creative enough for my kind of problem solving.

Molly's staring down at her notebook, taking notes as fast as Ms. Lewiston talks, and Ms. Lewiston is going at quite a clip. Molly must be literally writing every word.

Does she think there's going to be a quiz? Apparently over-achieving isn't something that Molly can turn on and off. If she's going to be in this Justice Circle, she's going to be the Best. Darn. Justice-Circle-Goer. EVER.

Then there's Alice, who appears to have disappeared to Aliceland. She finished crafting that black yarn thing and now is gazing at the ceiling, smiling like she knows some excellent secret, and moving her lips slightly while whispering to herself. She's so creepy it's almost awesome.

Andre is sitting totally still, staring to the right of Ms. Lewiston. His hands are in his lap, and the only part of him that's moving is his wrists, which look like they're doing some complicated patterns under his desk. I have to stop looking because staring at a dude's lap, even if he is a major nerd, is just asking for trouble.

Erik looks like he's about to start drooling. His heavy eyelids are doing those drop-and-pop-open-again moves that *come* before total head bobs. It would *so* delight my evil heart if he straight up fell asleep and smashed his head on the desk.

And Jax . . . if he didn't seem like the kind of guy who could potentially trash my photos for the LOLs, I might feel bad for him. He looks like he wants to do grievous harm to something or someone, or maybe himself. He'd *totally* gnaw off his leg if it were in a trap. Just a guess.

Finally Ms. Lewiston winds down. I feel bad for her. She *loves* this justice stuff—she's all fired up for us to use this experience as a way to grow and be braver and better people. But I mean, really, we are as checked out as it's possible to be while still in a circle with a fake candle and a bunch of special rocks. And come on. I've *done* my job. I agreed to show up. Isn't it up to them now? Don't they have to make it up to me and be all . . . I don't know . . . *just?*

CHAPTER 4

Bird Trauma and Farts Are Questionable Elements of a Justice Circle

There's a moment of silence, and I realize Ms. Lewiston has probably asked us something. Whoops.

"Okay. We're going to try something else," she says, her voice cheerful.

I wasn't aware we had tried anything at all yet. Guess I need to pay more attention.

"Everyone get out of your chair. Come on! Stand up, push the chairs back, and lie on the floor. Right on the floor." Ms. Lewiston starts us off, shoving her chair back with an unholy *screeeeeeeeeeeeeeeech* that makes Molly whimper, and lies right down. Her knee makes a crack like a popgun, but she doesn't complain.

"Um . . . the floor . . . isn't it kind of . . ." Molly, still firmly planted in her chair, wrinkles her nose.

"It's fine. I'm not asking you to lick it," Ms. Lewiston says, her voice the tiniest bit impatient.

I snort. I can't help it. Molly shoots me a death glare, and I stare back. Again, I mentally give her a shout-down that I'm doing everyone a solid by agreeing to spend my vacation here. She looks away, pushes her chair back, and slowly lowers herself, nose wrinkled in a fierce Everything Is Awful face. One by one everyone else clambers down.

"Heads in the middle, close together, like the rays of a sun," Ms. Lewiston calls. Her voice sounds a little flat from the floor.

I turn my head and quickly turn it back. I'm WAY too close to Alice's fake black eye for comfort. That thing looks completely real. Impressive, in a fairly disgusting way.

"Okay, we're going to close our eyes, and we're going to go around the circle, each of us saying one thing people don't know about us. This has nothing to do with Theo's photos," she adds, which is interesting, because I was about to ask what the heck this has to do with my photos.

But okay.

"I'll start," she continues, "and we'll go around from there. Jax, you can go next."

There's a moment of silence—well, not really silence, but no-voices quiet, where the only sounds are people squirming and breathing and the occasional *squirrrrk* of a sneaker against linoleum.

"I'm terrified of birds," Ms. Lewiston says suddenly. "Not in a funny way, but really frightened. When I was a kid, a magpie got into my kitchen and got caught in my hair. I still remember the strength of the wings flapping and hitting my face, the smell of bird poop, the sharp claws as it scrabbled around trying to get free. I really don't like them. They scare me."

Well. That's kind of intense.

Silence reigns supreme for a moment. Then of course . . .

Jax snorts, tries valiantly to make it sound like a sneeze, only to make the most pathetically fake sneeze sound in the history of pathetic fake sneezes—we're talking a full-on cartoon AAAAHHHHCHOO! Then he snorts again, then starts laughing.

Like a stack of cruel, helpless dominoes, we go down.

First Erik, then Alice, and finally Andre and me, who I thought was going to be mature in the face of it all, ultimately burst out with an explosive BHAAAAA! Even more tragically, the effort of trying to hold back the laugh was apparently too much for Molly's system, because she lets out a massive trumpeting fart at the same time.

At this Jax is totally gone. He rolls back and forth from stomach to back, kicking and flailing his arms like a baby.

No sound comes out of his throat, just a kind of choking, gasping that so often accompanies the best hysterical laughter.

Gaspsnortwheeze.

Gaspgaspgasp.

Snort.

I'm laughing so hard I don't hear the door open. But we all hear Ms. Davis just fine.

"Ms. Lewiston!"

That's all she says, but what is clearly expressed, without words, is:

1) WHAT THE @#$*$% IS HAPPENING HERE?
2) HOW IS THIS A JUSTICE CIRCLE?
3) IT'S NOT EVEN A CIRCLE.
4) I DID NOT AGREE TO GIVE UP MY SCHOOL VACATION WEEK AND THE SIMPLE ACT OF SUSPENDING FIVE KIDS FOR THIS RAMA-LAMA-DING-DONG EXERCISE.

Or something like that.

Ms. Lewiston sits up. Somehow seeing her sitting literally at the feet of Principal Davis, who, honestly, is a bit of a troll, makes me feel pretty bad.

"It was laughter therapy," I say, sitting up and brushing off my hands, which are gritty and gray with dust. Molly might have been on to something with her This Floor Is Going to Kill Us face. "Um. You know. Laughing to release emotion?"

Ms. Lewiston shoots me a complicated look. It might be "Thanks for having my back, home slice." But it might also be "Shut up, you're making it worse." Hard to tell with adults sometimes.

"No worries, Ms. Davis," she says, and her voice is pretty composed and cool, considering she's covered in school-floor-toxic-waste-or-maybe-just-lint and being mocked by seventh graders. "This is part of the process."

She pauses. "It's all part of the process," she repeats, and looks at Jax, who sat up and is staring at the floor. The laser force of her gaze could burn through most household objects and possibly titanium and platinum too. Jax looks at her, then proceeds to be fascinated with the ceiling.

Ms. Davis pauses for a minute, then delivers a final, threatening-sounding "I'll be checking back on the 'process' later. And I'll hope that it has led to a confession, rather than a waste of time and resources."

Then she stomps out of the room like a bad movie villain. I think she even wanted to slam the door, but of course it's one of those pressure-type doors that won't slam. Bummer for her.

When she's gone, Ms. Lewiston takes a deep breath. Silence, thick and uncomfortable, spreads.

Then, out of the corner of his mouth, Jax makes a quiet, barely audible *cawwww* sound. Like a bird.

Ms. Lewiston stands up, with a fairly impressive yoga lift from sitting, and holds out a hand to Jax. They leave the room in silence.

Wow. Welcome to the Justice Club.

The rest of us stare at each other in awkward silence. Then Alice leans forward. "Molly, if you want a Gas-X, I always have them in my bag. Help yourself. Irritable bowel syndrome is no joke."

And just like that I realize we haven't even scratched the surface of awkward.

CHAPTER 5

Lunchtime Is Interesting Only for How My Stomach Tries to Eat Itself

Things settle down after the great bird/laugh/fart/Davis meltdown. (Which, I have to say, is not a combination I ever thought would appear in a single sentence.)

Jax and Ms. Lewiston return, Jax quietly mumbles an apology to all of us about not respecting the process, and we lie back down in our circle. Ms. Lewiston once again asks us to tell something about ourselves that others don't know.

This is what people share. I'm totally blown away by the bravery people showed—if by "blown away" I mean "literally willing to be blown backward through a space-time continuum to avoid listening to such time-wasting garbage ever again in my life."

Molly states that she's allergic to every kind of animal fur.

Jax states that he freaking loves Wu-Tang Clan and that we should have an iPod in here.

Erik states that he once tried playing ice hockey and it was wicked cool, but then he committed to basketball.

Andre states that his family has moved five times.

I state that I'm saving up for a telephoto lens, but the one I want is four hundred dollars.

And Alice—well, there's always Alice. *She* shares plenty, that's for sure. We learn that:

1) She always wanted a hairless cat because they look elegant.
2) She's seen *Blair Witch Project* seven times.
3) She has a younger sister who does not like horror movies.
4) She's scared of ferrets.

Finally Ms. Lewiston has to interrupt her. "Thank you, Alice. That's fantastic that we get to learn so much about you. But we're going to stop sharing these facts and switch directions, okay?"

I almost wish she would let Alice keep going. . . . It's oddly soothing listening to her babble.

Then Ms. Lewiston asks us to think about something that makes us feel nervous or vulnerable. Not to say it out loud—she has to say this quickly, because it's clear Alice is about to let loose with what is sure to be a cosmically weird or embarrassing fact—but simply to think about it.

I don't want to do it, and, really, how's Ms. Lewiston going to know? I could be thinking about macro zoom lenses or cheese or *Doctor Who*. But like a magnet drawn to the true north of miserable memories, I think about my dad saying he still loves us but can't live this life anymore. And how he cried, but my mom and I didn't, and I had this weird idea that by not crying I was siding with her.

Gut punch.

I have no idea what my face looks like, but when I look around, I can see that at least some kids are following instructions, or at least they, like me, can't help themselves. Molly looks like she swallowed glass. I mentally roll my eyes. I've been in classes with Molly Claremont since kindergarten and Mrs. Gershuny's class. She always had coordinated outfits, lunch boxes with whatever Pixar-animated character was coolest, and, back when popularity was dictated in part by birthday celebrations, a parent who not only baked cupcakes but brought them in one of those special triple-decker cupcake-carrying containers. Because she had to be the best at everything in life, including Having the Most Cupcakes.

Ms. Lewiston speaks again, and her voice is soft. "Now,

I'm not going to ask you guys to share what you were thinking, but I hope you looked at each other. I mean really looked. Because I want you to remember one of my favorite quotes." She stands up and goes to the board. Taking a marker, she writes *Be kind, for all of us are fighting unseen battles.*

She turns to us, and says it out loud, slowly. "'Be kind, for all of us are fighting unseen battles.' Think about it. Think about what you might not know about each other, what others might not know about you."

We nod like we're pondering these great mysteries, but I suspect I'm not the only one who's thinking that my giant hot chocolate was a while ago and I need to pee like someone's squeezing my bladder.

As though she's reading my mind (awkward), Ms. Lewiston claps her hands. "Let's take a break to go to the bathroom, grab lunch, and stretch. Then we'll come back and circle up again."

Jax is out of his chair like someone used a catapult. I'm right behind him.

When I get back to the room, Ms. Lewiston's still gone. Judging from my time with her last year, I'm guessing she's in the teacher's lounge holding her mouth open under the coffee maker. That woman would have an IV drip of caffeine if she could.

Meanwhile, Molly is opening her backpack and settling in. She squirts sanitizer on her hands and rubs vigorously. Then she spreads out a cloth napkin and pulls out a bunch of tiny metal containers that all fit together, laying them out like they're fragments of an ancient scroll. As she opens them up and places the different foods on the napkin, I swear all I can think of are the old picture books I loved as a kid, about a badger named Frances. (Note: I didn't know Frances was a badger until around two years ago, when we gave some of these books to my cousins. Nathan asked me to read the badger book, and then his little sister Rachel went to find the book and bring it to me. And who knew? That weird black-and-white-striped creature? I guess it's a badger.)

ANYWAY. My point is that in those books, Frances has the most *epic* lunches. I'm talking six courses, complete with condiments and, if memory serves, a tiny vase of flowers for ambiance. Molly wasn't quite there, but she was close.

Next to her, Erik pulls up his chair and opens his backpack. He then proceeds to unwrap a cinder-block-size stack that turns out to be four sandwiches. Each one disappears in around three bites. I'm both disgusted and mesmerized. It's like seeing a snake unhinge its jaw and swallow a rodent whole.

Erik leans toward Molly. "Dude. This is so weak. I can't believe I'm missing ball camp for this."

Molly makes a noncommittal noise, her eyes flashing to me, then flicking away fast when she sees I'm listening. Good. Doesn't feel right to whine about being here? Doesn't seem like you're the victim? Exactly.

But Erik's oblivious, for something totally new and different. Like I said, just because he's never been *proven* to be a bully doesn't mean he doesn't join his Neanderthal bromates in nerd bashing when he has the chance. I mean, if one person hangs out with guys who regularly throw people's backpacks in the garbage, isn't he *slightly* more likely? Deductive Reasoning 101, right?

Molly lowers her voice. "I can't actually believe *I'm* a suspect." She cuts her eyes to Jax and Alice, then back to Erik. "You know?"

Erik doesn't answer, probably due to the half pound of processed lunch meat glued to the roof of his mouth, but he nods.

Molly continues. "I mean, why would *I* even care about his photos? It's so *wrong*!"

I lean back in my chair. I know exactly what she means. It goes against the laws of physics, aerodynamics, or at least the laws of Shipton Middle School. Why would top-of-the-food-chain people like Molly Claremont, of permanent honor roll fame, even bother with me?

I'm not the bottom of the food chain, the phytoplankton that can't even be seen. That would be Andre, who's invisible. And I'm not the oh-so-vulnerable clown fish, whose bizarre coloring helps shield it even while it stands out looking poisonous and weird; that would be Alice. And I'm not like Jax, who's like . . . I don't even know what. Maybe the hippo, or something that isn't carnivorous but manages to trash everything in its path regardless. And I'm certainly not, and never will be, Erik Estrale, Most Likely to Be in the Town Newspaper While Wearing a Mouthguard.

Before I can go any further down this accurate-but-depressing wormhole, Jax crashes back into the room.

"Man, was that you, Theo? Or Erik? The bathroom smells like someone took a monster-size deuce in the sink." He waves a hand in front of his face. "Nasty."

I ignore him. Like I'd poop at school. My lower intestine would have to be exploding first. But Molly's face closes up like a fist.

"Why do you have to be so *disgusting*, Jax? Seriously. Why would you need to tell us that?"

Jax straddles the back of his chair again and uses his foot to pull his backpack closer. "Oh, sorry, princess. Didn't realize you were so delicate. Must be hard for you, hearing about such things."

Molly scowls. "What are you talking about? I just don't want to hear about the smell of the boys' bathroom while I'm eating!"

"Yeah, because it's too much for you! Probably would be your worst nightmare."

Molly slams her hand down, hard. "You have. No. Idea. None. So shut up!"

Jax shrugs. "Whatever you say." He adjusts the flat brim of his hat and begins to unpack his lunch. Molly, Erik, and I all watch him unwrapping things like it's the most interesting show on TV.

He pulls out what looks like half a baguette with some kind of grilled meat and veggies in it, a container of raspberries, some fancy-looking rice crackers that look like artwork, and two cookies. Noticing us all staring, he raises his eyebrows so high they disappear under his hat.

"Can I *help* you?" he asks.

Molly turns away but not before she exhibits a spectacular nuclear-red blush. "No. Just . . . nice lunch."

Jax snorts. "Yeah. You sound surprised. You thought I'd have some *ghetto* lunch or something?"

We all freeze. Jax is African American, and Molly, Erik, and I aren't. (Andre is, but he doesn't hang with the pretty small group of black kids at school the way Jax does. Andre, like phytoplankton, doesn't really hang with anyone.) Jax, with his flattop and his fancy sneakers and his baggy pants, stands out a little. And now he looks at us like we're judging him. Suddenly all three of us are scrambling and babbling, trying to *not* sound like racist idiots.

Jax waits for us to wind down.

"Losers," he mumbles around a bite of his sandwich.

None of us answers.

My face is hot, and I'm unreasonably embarrassed. For a second I think I'll say something, but I reconsider, and what comes out is a kind of goat bleat, so I pretend I'm coughing and turn away. Who's he to get up in my face? I'm the one whose stuff was trashed.

I'm the victim here.

I let my hair fall on either side of my face and go back to my book, taking one last look at Jax's lunch.

My stomach growls a little, but I don't want to eat my granola bar or apple yet. Lesson learned: Today I packed a grudge lunch to protest being here. I'm now starving and tempted to bribe Jax or Molly for their food, which of course I won't do. I have a strict policy of flying solo, and begging for food definitely won't work. Jax gives a little grunt of pleasure as he bites into his sandwich, and a shower of flaky baguette crumbs rains down. I make myself turn away and look at Alice, who appears to be licking Fun Dip powder out of an open packet for her lunch, and Andre, who's silently eating from a thermos of soup. Luckily, or not, no one seems to care that my stomach is making an effort to eat itself. Even here, I don't really matter.

As I look around, the sheer weirdness of being stuck in a room with this particular group of five kids hits again. Every time I think about getting the phone call at home, being asked to return to school because there had been an "incident," and walking into the student gallery to the sight of my photographs destroyed feels like a punch to the solar plexus.

It was bad. It was so . . . *public*. All I wanted, then and now, was for the whole thing to disappear, vaporize without a trace, and leave me unscathed in the aftermath. But of course that isn't how it went down.

My list of "suspects" (said with an ironic set of air quotes because, really, this isn't *Law & Order*): Erik, as discussed, is a person of interest for sure. But next is Jax, probably, just because he's a loose cannon who's always getting in trouble. Who knows if he'd trash the art gallery, but I can't say he *wouldn't*. Then maybe Alice, because when you're that weird, you can't be counted out. Molly, who has been disgusted with me since kindergarten, is seriously unlikely, but who knows? It's possible my messy hair and drawn-on

Converse and ripped jeans offend her sense of order so cosmically she had to right the wrong. Andre? Honestly, unless he's got a secret life as a serial killer or something, I can't see it.

I shake my hair down in front of my face and stare at the floor. These five people in the room . . . they either ruined my photographs or saw someone else doing it and don't care enough to tell the truth. Someone in this room did a lot of work to hurt me. No, not me, my stuff. I'm fine. My self-portraits . . . not so much.

Still. It must have taken a while to scribble on every single image, to decide which awful words to write across them, to draw obscene body parts everywhere. Shows real commitment. And whoever did it was rewarded by it being the most dramatic act of vandalism at Shipton Middle School, ensuring everyone would talk about it. Afterward, everywhere I went, either I was immediately swarmed by do-gooder students who had their "somebody died" face going, or else people avoided me like my epic humiliation might be contagious.

I grab my apple and face the window, taking a huge bite. Whatever. I'm here to try to put this whole thing behind me as fast as I can, and that's it. Ms. Lewiston might want me to talk all about the hurt, but the fact is, whoever did it already trashed my stuff. I see no reason to let them see the additional damage.

CHAPTER 6

A Brief and Depressing
Trip Down Memory Lane

When Ms. Lewiston comes back, we circle back up and talk about personal responsibility and community. Reasonable topics. Sort of. Except not really.

> **Alice:** I think an example of community would be the special effects world. Because we all share techniques and post our successes but also are open and share our failures. The failures are *so* epic sometimes! (She begins to giggle maniacally. We all stare at our desks, avoiding eye contact.)
>
> **Ms. Lewiston:** Interesting, Alice. How did you find this community? Do you meet on weekends? Does Shipton Youth Services offer classes?
>
> **Alice:** OH! No! I've never met any of them!

I only know them on YouTube. There are whole channels dedicated to effects. KatherinetheRad is one of my faves. And Grommet—he's awesome. But I think he lives in Munich or something.

I can't tell you what happens next, because my mind is filled with images of an angsty German dude named Dieter who wears a black turtleneck sweater and films endless videos of himself with fake head wounds.

Anyway, by the time the day wraps up, even Ms. Lewiston looks a little worn out. I realize that I literally can't remember if Andre has said a word since he told us his family has moved five times. And I also realize that Molly hasn't spoken since lunch. As Ms. Lewiston tells us to get packed up, I look over and Molly hasn't moved.

I kick the leg of her chair. "Hey. Are you listening? We can pack up." I don't know why I care, except that her face ... There's a poem my mom read me (she's always reading me poetry ... she says it's better out loud) about some old-fashioned damsel who's under a curse. It's called "The Lady of Shalott," and there's this line in it:

> *The mirror crack'd from side to side*
> *"The curse has come upon me!" cried*
> *The Lady of Shalott.*

Molly looks like that. Like she just got cursed or some-thing. But as soon as the quote pops into my mind, her face dissolves into a far more typical Everything Is Disgusting expression, and I think I imagined the whole thing. Except that her hands are trembling a little as she packs up her bag and jams a wool hat with a giant pom-pom onto her head.

I stand up. I file Molly under Not My Problem. Maybe she's thinking about all the extra-credit work she can't get done this week. Maybe she's worried that she doesn't have coordinated socks for the outfit she planned tomorrow. Who knows? Who cares?

We all shuffle out of the room and down the hallway toward the front exit. My mom swore that she'd try to be here on time, but . . . yeah. Her definition of "on time" is within a cool twenty-minute window of the target.

Sure enough, when we get out there, there's a shiny black Volvo SUV, a newish but filthy silver minivan, and a sleek gold Lexus waiting on the curb. Molly slides into the SUV, which has windows tinted so dark I can't even see who's driving. Jax climbs into the back of the minivan, which has loud kids' music and some cheerful bellowing going on inside. A white dude is driving, and he seems to be attempting to talk on the phone, pass the loud kid a snack cup, and greet Jax simultaneously. Jax ignores him and hits the button to close the door. Alice, who removed her black eye during lunch, gets into the Lexus, which pulls away almost before she closes the door.

Andre and Erik both look at me, then at each other.

"Well, gotta dip. Going to see if I can make the last hour of camp, then hit the gym. You know what they say, 'You can't win the game if you're not *in* the game!'"

I actually didn't know they said that. I don't even know who *they* are. I don't care either. The last thing I need is Erik's fake friendliness. It's like having a hyena wanting to hang out, chat, while you, an impala, sit there, nursing a broken leg. As we're talking, Andre slips away and is halfway down the block before Erik finishes yapping. The boy is STEALTH. I spend a productive few minutes imagining Andre as some kind of spy assassin who hides his mad skill beneath ironed jeans and plaid shirts. But then I get bored.

Fifteen minutes after everyone else leaves, there's still no sign of my mom. I love her, I really do. We have an awesome relationship, especially considering that it's just the two of us these days. She's funny and talks to me like a real human and not a tweenbot, and she tells hilarious stories, and she laughs at my jokes—serious SNORT-LAUGH laughing, not pity laughing—and she's a librarian, so we always have awesome books, including advance copies. But the woman is not exactly watching the clock.

My brain spins backward in time, like those old-school movies where newspapers flip back to a date in the past. Given my mom's track record, I probably have enough time to go back to my conception. But that's (1) disgusting and (2) not really relevant here.

I *do* go back as far as the last week of summer vacation before sixth grade, because . . . REASONS. Family reasons. And even though it's only vaguely related to the whole Justice Circle disaster, compared with staring at the same suspicious brown stain on the pavement, it seems like the lesser of two evils.

Events Leading Up to This Mildly Tragic Justice Circle (In Reverse Order)

15. Ms. Lewiston thought suspending five students who may or may not have been involved in an act of vandalism and destruction was not cool.

14. Due to the school policy of zero tolerance for vandalism, Ms. Davis wanted to suspend the five students found in the art gallery in the wake of the epic destruction there, especially after my pinhole cameras were subsequently ruined in the darkroom.

There's zero tolerance for a lot of things at our school. Ms. Davis is big on zero tolerance.

13. None of the five who were in the gallery had an alibi for when the darkroom door was opened.

12. No one was caught.

11. Two days ago, one day after the gallery debacle, someone opened the door to the darkroom, where my long-exposure pinhole cameras were, and ruined them.

10. No one admitted to doing anything, seeing anything, or knowing anything.

9. At 5:50 p.m. Molly Claremont walked into the gallery and started screaming that it had been vandalized. She was joined almost immediately by Alice Shu, who had just walked in; Erik Estrale, who was right outside the door that leads to the cafeteria; Jax Fletcher, who was walking by the other door toward the gym; and (maybe) Andre Hall, whose bag was in the gallery but who swears he was in the bathroom until after Ms. Davis showed up.

8. Three days ago my large-form self-portraits, hung elegantly (if unwillingly) in the student gallery space, were "defaced," which is a polite word for "someone scribbled military-grade nastiness all over them."

7. Three weeks ago, with the encouragement of Mr. Smith (photography teacher) and Ms. Lewiston (future Justice Circle leader), I somewhat reluctantly agreed to hang my large-form self-portraits in the student gallery the week before February break.

6. Last spring my photographs won an honorable mention in our town's "Winter Imagery" contest.

5. Last year for Christmachanukah (Jewish mom, Christian dad) I got my first serious camera.

4. At the start of sixth grade I reallyreallyreally didn't want to come to school, so my mom and Ms. Lewiston came up with the idea of my being the school archivist, which was a nice way of giving me a reason to stand on the sidelines of everything and take pictures.

3. The week before sixth grade started, my dad left.

2. My dad used to travel a lot, and would send me lots of photos.
1. I was born.

So that's pretty much it. After it all went down, Ms. Lewiston went hard, asking me to please "go high when they go low" and "rise above the easy answers" to "do the hard work of making things better."

Frankly, it's a lot to ask. What I really want is for this whole thing to go away. I keep reminding myself that they're just photos. And let's be honest: most people in this school wouldn't know good art if it landed on their heads while wearing a Viking helmet. Every time the horrible aliens-in-my-stomach-threatening-to-erupt feeling hits, I breathe deep, Mom's-yoga-style, and tell myself that I'm fine, that I don't ever—and I mean *ever*—have to live through this again.

Ms. Lewiston keeps saying she knows I'm being strong about it, but that's not it. I put my artwork out there and it was a huge mistake. My photos will not be displayed in public again until I'm long gone from Shipton. Knowing that it would take high-level torture to make me repeat this egregious error in judgment is comforting somehow, since I can't envision a scenario where that happens.

So yeah, I don't want to go high. I prefer to go snarky,

honestly. But Ms. Lewiston is probably the best thing I have going at school, and even though she wouldn't say it, or at least I don't think she would, I know that she and Ms. Davis are often doing their moose-charging dance, and this justice thing is important to her.

I'm debating the wisdom of trying to call my mom—she refuses to answer the phone while driving, so if I *do* call, she'll simply pull over somewhere to answer, thus slowing the pace of her arrival from snail-crawling-uphill to glacial. But before I can weigh the pros and cons, the front door opens with a bang, and Ms. Davis flies out. Ms. Lewiston comes out right behind her.

"I think it's safe to say that if what I saw was an indication, this process is a waste of time and money," Davis snaps, her voice devoid of all the syrupy sweetness she uses on the kids. Clearly, she doesn't see me slumped on the bench by the wall. "I'm tempted to pull the plug now, rather than lose a full week—"

"Lose a week of what?" Ms. Lewiston asks. Her voice is chill, but she's got a pretty solid tell for when she's cheesed: one eyebrow goes up almost to her hairline, while the other stays still.

"A full week of *my* much-needed and well-deserved vacation, for one!" Davis says. "You realize that while you've given your time, I also need to be here."

Ms. Lewiston shrugs. "I'm sorry that it's inconvenienced you. The kids' families have all agreed that this is a worthwhile process, and they're committed to it. As I've said before, the goal is to establish trust before pushing for answers. This is about more than just victims and perpetrators." Then, in a seriously advanced maneuver, she swerves around and ahead of Davis so there can be no eye contact. "I'm looking forward to engaging them tomorrow and moving forward."

But Davis actually pulls Ms. Lewiston's arm, holding her back. "That's fine," she snaps. "But bear in mind that this . . . process . . . is your responsibility. And if it fails to deliver results—and by results I do mean an admission of guilt and appropriate punishment—then your next performance review will be the place we discuss it. And I don't think I have to remind you that budgets are tighter than ever. We're finalizing next year's numbers, and staffing constraints are already an issue."

I almost expect Davis to disappear in a puff of green smoke after this, but no, she mutters something about opposite-side parking for street cleaning tomorrow, and the need to stop at Home Depot, then unlocks a poop-colored sedan with a Support State Troopers bumper sticker and drives away. Man. What an anticlimax. She can't even be a decent villain.

Ms. Lewiston stands still for a second, staring out into space. Then she mutters a word that she definitely would not repeat if she knew I was within earshot and stomps off toward her car. Unlike the Wicked Witch of the Front Office's, Ms. Lewiston's car isn't in front of the school, but stuck with the peasants' along the side.

There is approximately a 1 million percent chance that this school without Ms. Lewiston would be an abyss of boringness. Apparently, I *will* have to make this Justice Circle work, or at least not let it go down in flames. This depressing realization hits right as my mom screeches into the parking lot.

"SORRY! So sorry, love! Sorrysorrysorry. There was one last phone call that I thought would be quick but . . ." Mom blathers on, and I smile and tell her it's all good, that I wasn't waiting long (lie). But meanwhile, in my head I'm working over one thought: that this better end well. Because as much as this week is a trash fire of epic proportions, Ms. Lewiston getting canned would be far worse.

CHAPTER 7

Day Two Assessments

Date: Feb. 19

Name: *Molly Claremont*

What happened and what were you thinking at the time of the incident?
Didn't I already answer this?? I HAVE NO IDEA.

What have you thought about since?
I want to help. I really do. But yesterday was literally the worst school day I've ever spent. I can't do this all week.

What about this has been hardest for you?
Um. See above?

What do you think needs to be done to make things as right as possible?

Is there any data to support the idea that locking the six of us in a room is going to lead anywhere? I mean, sure, I'm all for finding out who did this and punishing him (because it's not me, and seriously, does anyone think it's Alice? She IS super weird, but still).

Is there anything at all you'd like to share confidentially with Ms. Lewiston?

I want this whole thing to end. I need it to be over.

Name: Andre Hall

What happened and what were you thinking at the time of the incident?

Still wasn't there when it happened. Still wish someone had noticed that I wasn't there so I could get out of this.

What have you thought about since?

Not much. Yesterday was kind of a waste of time. Though Alice's makeup effects are pretty intense.

What about this has been hardest for you?

When I got home last night my bandmates were wiped out from an all-day session. I asked if they'd hold off today and start later so I can join. If this goes on I'm going to lose my band.

What do you think needs to be done to make things as right as possible?

We need someone to admit they did it so the rest of us can get out of here.

Is there anything at all you'd like to share confidentially with Ms. Lewiston?

Is it possible someone knows that I wasn't there, but doesn't want to say it out loud?

Name: *Erik Estrale*

What happened and what were you thinking at the time of the incident?

Look, it wasn't me. Like I said, I was thinking about the game against Greenfield. They have a wicked offense, and their center is a freaking giant. So hard to guard. But no idea about the photos.

What have you thought about since?
Yesterday was kind of a trip, man. Molly let one
RIP. Hilarious.

What about this has been hardest for you?
Coach had left and locked up the gym yesterday
when I tried to join the camp. I did a ten-mile run,
but not sure that's enough. No pain, no gain.

**What do you think needs to be done to make things as
right as possible?**
No idea, but I'm not sure it's going to happen in this
room.

**Is there anything at all you'd like to share confidentially
with Ms. Lewiston?**
What if someone tells, but there's no proof? What
happens then? Just curious.

Name: Alice Shu

**What happened and what were you thinking at the
time of the incident?**
My answer hasn't changed since yesterday.

What have you thought about since?

Well, I've thought about a ton of different things since that day. This is a really imprecise question, you know? You don't want me to list everything I've thought about since, do you? That would take ages.

What about this has been hardest for you?

Not sure, but I will say I've been a little obsessed about the idea of Ms. Lewiston getting attacked by a magpie. I kind of want to make a movie of it.

What do you think needs to be done to make things as right as possible?

I wonder if Theo is at all glad we're doing this. That IS the point, right?

Is there anything at all you'd like to share confidentially with Ms. Lewiston?

This isn't a school where people feel safe telling the truth, I don't think.

Name: Jax Fletcher

What happened and what were you thinking at the time of the incident?

SAME ANSWER

What have you thought about since?

SAME ANSWER

What about this has been hardest for you?

SAME ANSWER

What do you think needs to be done to make things as right as possible?

SAME ANSWER

Is there anything at all you'd like to share confidentially with Ms. Lewiston?

SAME ANSWER SAME ANSWER SAME ANSWER

CHAPTER 8

Present-Day Theo Would Like to Go Back and Slap Past Theo Across the Face. Hard.

Day two, Justice Circle. If I were a scientist, my observations would be the following: The subjects appear agitated, sullen, unconcerned, and . . . possibly asleep. Some seem to be dreading the impending psychological battering, while others exhibit symptoms of denial.

It should be noted that the subject known as Alice is currently sporting a nail coming out of the back of her right hand. It should also be noted that all other subjects are trying to check it out without being caught checking it out. It should finally be noted that it looks freaking *sick,* and I kind of want to photograph it.

Ms. Lewiston comes in a few minutes after we all settle down. She's carrying a massive coffee urn masquerading as a cup. I've seen bathtubs smaller than that thing. I wish I had thought to bring coffee too, but my mom had the travel mug filled with her gross chai stuff. She promised to get us another mug, but somehow every time we go to Target, the bill is $300 before we even get to the fancy cat food we have to buy so Otis doesn't puke it all up, and I quietly shove the stuff we can't afford into the magazine rack. (Sorry, Target employees who find the thermos, ironic Captain America T-shirt, organic catnip toy, and other abandoned items I leave there. My bad.)

Anyway, the smell coming off Lewiston's coffee is enough to give me a contact buzz, so I close my eyes and inhale deeply.

Molly gives an irritated sigh. Then another one. It's messing with my caffeine fantasies, so I open my eyes and glare at her.

"What's the problem? This whole thing cutting into your social schedule?"

She glares back in a way that makes it clear she is exactly as interested in Justice Circles as she is in head lice.

I'm about to make a comment about how she must be desperate to send a Snapchat before she gets the shakes from withdrawal when I remember her hands actually *were* shaking yesterday. My mouth was already open to snark, and I close it again, probably resembling a largemouth bass. I do it a few more times, like I was exercising my jaw. Because *that's* more normal. Just Theo, doing his jaw exercises. Like he does. I stop.

She looks at me. "What?" she says, and her voice is suspicious.

"Nothing." I glance at Ms. Lewiston, who is staring into her coffee cup like it holds the mysteries of the universe. "Just . . . you know. Sorry your vacation week is screwed up."

Molly, if possible, looks more annoyed. Her cheeks flame red, and for a second I remember Alice wanting to do special effects bruises on her, and Molly's horrified look.

Annnnnnnd . . . my good deed detonates as I snort-laugh in Molly's face. Even when I'm trying *not* to be a total snarky tool, I fail. Miserably. I mentally punch myself in the kidney a few times.

"Sorry! I wasn't . . . I swear I'm not laughing at you. I was remembering . . . Well. Never mind. But it wasn't at you."

Before I even finish talking, I know that, though it's a noble attempt, it's doomed to fail. Molly looks like she could spit nails.

"What. Ever."

List of things I wish existed in the world:

1) A DSLR camera that also shoots great video, fits in a pocket, and is waterproof.

2) A magic money tree in the backyard. (Note: When he still lived with us, my dad used to always say, "What, the car's busted again? Good thing we have that magic money tree!" And for years I believed him. Yet another cruel awakening. See also: Tooth Fairy.)

3) A way to not laugh at inappropriate times. See also: my dad telling me he was moving to Central America; Nonna's funeral; right now.

Ms. Lewiston takes a last desperate gulp of her coffee, then sets it down with a clank and claps her hands.

I look up, because, while this is definitely a World's Worst Vacation Week for me, it's no treat for Ms. Lewiston, who is not only *also* spending her vacation week here but has Davis the Humorless Zero Tolerance Troll on her back. I try to make an expression that says I'm both willing to be a part of this process and also I should under no circumstances be called on, because I don't really feel *that* bad for Ms. Lewiston. She shoots me a startled look, and I'm guessing that my expression is more like I'm fighting major indigestion or an internal demon for possession of my soul. Finally I give up and settle for low-grade sullen.

"Okay, good morning, everyone," Ms. Lewiston says once everyone stops shuffling and whispering and, yes, staring at the nail in Alice's hand. "I really hope that you all got some rest and a chance to think about this Justice Circle and what we're doing here. I think the first thing I'd like to do, if you're willing, is to get out of here."

She stands up.

I should mention that while I'm looking at her, doing my demonically possessed/passing gas/sullen face, everyone else is staring at the floor. At this, five heads pop up like someone yanked them on hooks.

"Where are we going? Are we leaving school?" Jax asks, pushing out of his chair so hard it falls backward. "Sweet, Ms. L. I like it."

"We can't leave school. That's against policy unless our parents agree. Remember when Mr. Ringel thought it would be cool to walk down to the river with the eighth graders for science? Everyone got in so much trouble. Ethan didn't even have an EpiPen with him."

This of course from Molly, who I suspect has internalized the Student Handbook to the point where I almost want to quiz her, *Jeopardy!*-style. "Give me Cafeteria Policies for two hundred, Theo!"

"Sorry, Jax, but we're staying in the building. So there's nothing to worry about, Molly. Actually, we're going to the library."

Jax gives a barely audible grunt that rhymes with *strap,*

but the rest of us are moderately excited. The school library was recently totally redone with couches, beanbags, and rugs, and some of us (i.e., nerds) spend a lot of time there, chilling out after lunch or "doing research" (i.e., avoiding alpha males like Erik's friends who like to engage in physical wedgie humor) during recess.

As we trudge through the empty hallways, we walk right by the student gallery, where my photos once hung. Even now, days later, I still get that sweaty-sick feeling looking at it. It was so surreal, walking into school that night, my mom charging in all mama-grizzly-on-the-attack. Everything faded away ... Davis's babbling, my mom's angry questions, even the stares and whispers of the remaining students, so that all that I could process was the art itself. Knocked sideways, ripped, one with a giant bronze Sharpie zigzag all over it that almost could have been artistic, if not for the words scrawled over and over. I ran into the bathroom and puked, puked out my after-school snack of Sun Chips and yogurt, puked out my lunch, puked out every single thing inside me, hard and fast. I was back before my mom was even done yelling.

And the thing is, I *knew* it was a bad idea to hang them. I mean, not because they weren't good. They were. Not saying that to be an arrogant turd, but I worked really hard on the lighting and did all this research into what portrait photographers like Annie Leibovitz do to make her images so dramatic.

But look. I'm not an idiot. I know that giant artsy black-and-white photographs of me, hair down, fedora on, was a face begging for a slap. *My* face, and the slap came in the form of graffiti that I still sometimes see in the minutes before I fall asleep.

It should be noted that even when you *know* something is a bad idea, even when you think you're expecting the worst, even when you're sure you're being realistic about the risks, it still hurts like *whoa* when the slap comes.

And of course Davis the Impaler *HELD AN ASSEMBLY,* because research clearly shows that idiot tweenbots are always really moved to tears by an assembly. Picture the flaccid and tragic school counselor rambling on about . . . yes, zero tolerance, and no place for hate, and have a friend, be a friend, and if you see something, say something. Then add the Davis-Troll-No-Tolerance speech, delivered in a shrill yowl.

Obviously, the whole student body was so moved that they stood up as one to cheer me on and to assure me that my work was valued and that I was a special member of the school community. Only it sounded like they were saying

I was a freak and a snitch and a loser and so *gay* (one of my favorites, really, because of course nothing says "sexually attracted to the same gender" like taking photographs, amirite?).

So, sort of the same thing, but not really.

What truly made the whole thing catastrophically stupid is that before this, I was left alone. I wasn't cool, or popular, but I had a few other loner types to sit with at lunch (Malcolm and Reese) and text with if I forgot an assignment (Mateo) and partner with in science or even the dreaded PE. These are not actual friends, of course. I don't really have them. But I fit in comfortably enough. I didn't hate school, at least. And while I wasn't surrounded by friends, I also wasn't one of those super-vulnerable kids who seem to get a nonstop stream of what I call mosquito-level bullying. I'm talking about the ones who are laughed at when they dare raise their hands, or have their backpacks thrown on top of the huge bookshelves so that the janitor has to get a ladder to retrieve them. Or the ones who find themselves sitting on ketchup packets on the bus. We're not talking after-school-special bullying, but still. It goes on all the time, and every time, I say a little prayer of gratitude to the gods of anonymity that I get left alone.

Then, after the photos went up and got publicly annihilated, it was like there was a spotlight on me. It was whispers of *"That's him. OMG, poor Theo,"* or *"Did you HEAR what they wrote? I would DIE,"* or *"Dude, thanks to Gustav's loser pictures getting trashed, there are teachers freaking everywhere."*

My sort-of-friendly-but-not friends were freaked out and didn't want to be targeted by association. (Except Mateo, who got a little too fired up about revenge and retaliation, and I had to start leaving lunch early so I didn't have to hear the plans for the overthrow of the ruling class.)

But it's school, and there's always some new drama erupting like a zit on Kevin Hellson's forehead. (Seriously, his last one was the size of a volcano. The dude should see a dermatologist. I'd feel bad for him except he's a total jerk, the star of the basketball team, and the kind of guy who calls things "gay" when he really means "clean and not covered in pictures of eagles clutching the American flag.") I guess the point of all this rambling is, people would have eventually moved on, and, without a real culprit or additional information, Davis might have given up.

Then I set up some cool long-exposure pinhole cameras in the darkroom, with the lighting set up just right, and got permission from Mr. Smith to come back in an hour and finish them. But between the time I closed the door and the time I went back, someone had opened the darkroom door. The door that I'd stuck a huge sign on that said, "Do. Not.

Open. (No seriously, DON'T OPEN THIS DOOR. Yes, I'm talking to you!)" And my prints were ruined. And it looked like I was being . . . what's the word? Ah yes. Targeted. Or maybe *bullied*.

And here we are.

I never should have hung those photos in the first place. Now Present-Day Theo would really like to go slap Past Theo across the face repeatedly. But I guess it's too late for that.

CHAPTER 9

A Spoonful of High-Fructose Corn Syrup Helps the Lies Come Out

When we get to the library, Ms. Lewiston leads us over to the nook, a pretty excellent area with a fake tree built up the wall and overhanging the couches and beanbags. Four-year-old me would have thought he died and went to heaven at the sight of this magic tree house/reading space, but honestly? Thirteen-year-old me is still pumped about it.

The great irony of this coziness is that it's usually empty. The school got a big grant to make the library so great, and some fancy interior designer donated her time to create the plans for the space. But now that it's finished, Davis is so uptight about the possibility of someone trashing it that she makes us get signed passes to sit on the couches. Yes, that's right. We need permission to sit down on the couches that the school so proudly purchased for us.

But Ms. Lewiston obviously believes in total anarchy,

or maybe she's just tired (she left the bathtub of coffee behind), and she gestures around her before tucking her legs up under her on the couch. (Another no-no; to quote Davis: "You can put your feet on the furniture in your own homes, I don't care! I don't care how you treat your houses. But not here! These couches are your legacy! You'll be leaving them for the next students who come through!")

Ms. Lewiston clearly does not care about our legacy.

Once again our seating pattern feels like one of those inkblot tests shrinks give people to figure out if they're crazy. Or at least, they do in movies. The shrink I saw after my dad left didn't show me any inkblots, but he did show me some really funny cartoons and also suggested an F-Bomb journal, where I could write down all the really awful things I would never say to my dad or mom or even him. He was cool.

Anyway, Molly sits next to Ms. Lewiston on the couch but keeps her feet on the ground. Her body language is clearly saying, "Seriously? Can you not even *sit* without all kinds of code infractions?"

Jax has face-planted in a beanbag, Erik is sitting on the arm of another couch (Rule Violation #2, as arm sitting is "disrespectful to the furniture"; I could not even make this up if I tried).

Anyway, Alice is sitting in a yoga full-lotus pose on a round ottoman, and Andre's in a small armchair, sitting quietly like ... well, like an advertisement for how to sit quietly in a chair. If anyone needed to advertise that for some reason.

"This is a little more comfortable, don't you think?" Ms. Lewiston asks. "I'm hoping as we get our bodies out of the classroom, we might be able to also break out of our shells a bit. What do you say?"

She looks around, and I'd love to say I look back eager and ready to open up, but after my last attempt at the listening-but-not-talking face I've decided to opt for a blank stare.

"And to get us started, I have another idea." Ms. Lewiston rustles around in her big leather purse and pulls out a glorious yellow-and-red bag we all know and love.

"Starburst!" Molly says, and I will say that she sounds happier than I have ever, and I mean *ever,* heard her. She quickly turns the color of the pink Starbursts (for the experts among us, that would be strawberry). "But no food's allowed in the library!"

"Special dispensation from Ms. Cody," Lewiston says, ripping open the bag. The delectable smell of high-fructose corn syrup and red dye number 40 wafts over us. "These are gluten-, dairy-, and nut-free, and they can't spill or make too much of a mess. We just have to throw out the wrappers."

Jax rolls around on the beanbag until he's on his knees, begging. "Don't tease! What do we gotta do to get those?"

Unless I'm mistaken, and I rarely am, everyone—even Andre, who has leaned forward a whole two inches—wants to know the answer to this.

"You're going to have to earn them," Ms. Lewiston says. "You're going to have to talk."

Jax leans back like he's been gut punched and yells in mock horror, "No!"

"Yes! But don't worry. I'm starting out with an easy one." Ms. Lewiston fishes around in the bag and closes her hand around one. "No peeking on the color," she says sternly to Molly, who leans over.

Molly moves up from strawberry to the full cherry-Starburst deep red, but she leans back.

"Okay, here's the first question. Tell us one time when you lied. It can be recent, it can be when you were a little kid, doesn't matter."

Silence.

"Does it matter if we got caught?" Jax asks.

Ms. Lewiston shakes her head.

"How will you know we're not lying now? What if I lie

to you about my lie, and that's my telling you about a lie? What then?" Jax continues.

Ms. Lewiston gives him that look that certain excellent adults have mastered; a look that says, basically:

1) I like you.
2) However, I'm on to whatever shenanigans you're trying to pull.
3) I don't want to go all Genghis Khan on your butt.
4) But I will.

Jax nods thoughtfully, like she made a fascinating statement about climate change or the Boston Celtics. "Right. Never mind," he says.

I look around. This is interesting. On one hand, greed and avarice. On the other, self-preservation. I sort of wish I had some Starburst to eat while watching this play out.

But Molly raises her hand.

Somewhere, a Russian judge is giving her top points for guts.

"When I was six, I stole a Hershey bar from Seven-Eleven. I didn't get caught, but when I got home, my baby-sitter saw it and asked when I got it. I told her someone gave it to me, but she didn't believe me. She asked again and again and finally told me she had seen me take it and was waiting for me to tell the truth. She made me bring it back to the store and apologize." She falls silent.

"That sounds really embarrassing," Alice says, her voice, as always, a little too loud.

Molly looks up, her face ready to be mad and You Are an Idiot–like, but Alice looks sympathetic. Or maybe Molly's just distracted again by the nail sticking out of Alice's hand. She nods. "Yeah. It was. I begged my babysitter not to tell my parents. I swore I'd never do it again."

With a theatrical whoosh, Ms. Lewiston pulls her hand out of the bag.

"Light pink! The best," Molly breathes.

"Did your babysitter tell?" Alice asks.

All our eyes are drawn to the unwrapping, but I'm curious too.

Molly looks up and locks eyes with Alice for a second, then looks away. "No. She never told them," she says. And something in her voice makes me wonder.

Ms. Lewiston smiles. "Thanks, Molly. For being brave enough—or hungry enough—to go first. Who's next?"

"Me!" Jax waves a hand in the air. "Also if you find yourself with a red one—"

"No special orders, Jax," Ms. Lewiston says. "But go for it. You've got the floor."

Jax leans back in the beanbag, which rustles and crinkles so loudly we can barely hear him. He speaks up to the ceiling.

"This summer I was messing around, and I made a slingshot out of a perfect piece of wood. I was testing it out, but by accident I flung a rock right at our neighbor's window, and it shattered."

He falls silent for a second, then keeps going.

"Well, he was out of town, which I knew, because we were taking care of his dog. And nobody had seen it. So I just . . . never told. When he came home from vacation and his window was broken, he was pretty freaked out and wound up calling and getting an alarm system installed, because he thought maybe someone had been planning to break in."

We're all silent. There's no fake toughness in Jax's voice, and Ms. Lewiston leans forward and hands him a yellow Starburst.

"You weren't expecting that, I'm sure," she says. "What did that feel like?"

"Bad," Jax says. "But by the time I knew he'd gotten the alarm and everything, I couldn't really see the point of telling the truth. What's he gonna do? Cancel and tell them to come uninstall it all? Naw . . . it was too late."

"Well, I guess it depends. Too late for him not to get an

alarm system, maybe. Though I will say often those alarm companies charge a monthly fee, so it might still be worth it for him to cancel. But there's also another potential goal that it's not too late for."

Jax shrugs. "Yeah? What?"

"Well, do you like your neighbor? Did you feel bad about his window?" Ms. Lewiston asks.

Jax shrugs again. "I mean, I guess. Yeah." He pauses. "Yeah, he's actually a really cool old dude."

"So the other goal might simply be to say you're sorry. To tell him it was an accident and you didn't mean any harm."

"What's the point of that? It'll get me in trouble, and the window's already been fixed and now he's got an alarm system. Nothing's going to be better because I got yelled at," Jax says.

But Ms. Lewiston smiles. "Point might be not to feel bad. That's enough of a reason, right?"

Before Jax can say anything more, she looks around. "Anyone else ready?"

Alice puts her hand up. "When I was in third grade, I saw Jennifer Malone had new Hello Kitty markers, and I really, really, REALLY wanted them. So during snack I took them and put them in my winter boots in my cubby. Later that day Jennifer couldn't find them, and we had to search the whole classroom. I pretended to help look, and when Mrs. Coates asked me if I had seen them, I said of course not, but I guess I'm not a very good liar, because she immediately made me go out in the hall and tell her where I put them. So I told her Jennifer had stolen the markers from me first, and I was stealing them back. Then I had to go to the principal's office."

There's a meditative silence as we all ponder this brave but ultimately doomed tactic.

"I remember that, actually," Erik says. "We had to stay in from second recess, and we had reserved the foursquare court. That was you? Why did you take them in the first place? There were, like, a million markers in Mrs. Coates's classroom."

Molly and Alice both look at Erik like he's got a jockstrap on his head.

"Hello Kitty markers are different," Molly says in her You Are Too Stupid to Live voice. "But I still wouldn't have stolen them."

"Unless they were made of chocolate," Erik mutters, and if I'm not mistaken, Andre snickers a little at that one.

"Anyway, I had to apologize to Jennifer, so I made her a whole foldout card—I was really into origami at the time— and she was cool about it. We actually were pretty good friends for the rest of that year; though when she invited me over for a sleepover, she made me promise not to steal anything." She's silent for a second. "So that was awkward."

Ms. Lewiston tosses her an orange Starburst.

"So we have people lying because they don't want to get in trouble, and lying because they wanted something they couldn't have without taking it. What are some other reasons people lie? Andre? Erik?" She turns toward me. "Theo? What about you?"

I think about what I might say. I lie fairly often, I guess. Not like pathological-level lying, but I'd say it's one of my better skills. I can lie about forgetting homework: "I swear I did it. I can see it sitting on my dining room table where I left it. Can I hand it in tomorrow?"

I lie about cookies: "Mom. Why would I lie about this? I only had two. I swear."

And, if needed, I lie about how I'm feeling. Because after months of watching your mom bite the inside of her lip and turn away and stare out the window (a window, I might add, that looks out at absolutely nothing), you learn to say "Fine, Mom. I'm fine." And sound like you mean it.

None of these are lies I feel like talking about. Still, I raise my hand.

"Theo! What you got?" Ms. Lewiston rustles her hand in the bag intentionally, like a signal.

If she keeps it up, we'll be drooling on command, Pavlov's dog–style.

"I told my younger cousins that a sand fairy left them magical seashells, but it was actually me," I say.

Ms. Lewiston looks disappointed. "I don't think that's really the same thing, Theo," she says, and even though her voice is chill, I get a little of the prickly hot-sweaty-embarrassed feeling.

"No? Seems like a lie to me. Seems like looking into the big bright eyes of a six-year-old and pinkie-swearing that, yes, a fairy magically came up out of the sea to leave them a gift is a big. Fat. LIE."

"Do you think telling made-up stories that feed the imagination is the same as lying?" Ms. Lewiston asks.

I want to sound funny, but when I speak, my voice is almost trembling. I stand up, suddenly too frustrated to sit still.

"Well, if you make a kid believe something and that something is NOT TRUE, then I think that's pretty much the definition of lying to someone's face. And let's be clear ... the next time they went to the beach, when I wasn't around, no magical fairy was going to be there."

"You don't know that." This is Alice, of course.

I'm almost glad she's volunteered to be her weird self right at this moment. It gives my frustration a target to point at.

"Yes, Alice, I do know. Because—spoiler alert!—fairies aren't real!" I'm being rude, and I don't even care. Usually Alice is someone I wouldn't be nasty to, since it's kind of like kicking a kitten, all wide eyes and confusion. But right now it doesn't matter. She's in front of me, practically volunteering.

She shakes her head. "Yah. Duh. But maybe it wasn't a lie. Maybe it was the beginning of magic. Maybe someone else—a parent or another older cousin or someone—hid a shell next time. Or maybe there was no shell, so one of them was disappointed, but the other one made up a story about how the sand fairy got waylaid by an evil octopus and couldn't deliver the shell. But then she went back to her fairy friends, and they worked together on a magical net that would capture the evil octopus."

We all contemplate this, and I take a few deep breaths until I don't feel like punching a wall.

"That's actually a wicked cool story," Erik says. "But probably the evil octopus could rip the net."

"Maybe," Alice says. "But either way, it works. My point is, you started the story, but someone else might pick it up. Stories sometimes have a life of their own."

Erik nods vigorously, because I'm sure he spends all his free time making up fairy stories, once he finishes bench-pressing nerds with his jock friends. I want to slap him, and

I force myself to take a deep breath. I'm usually not a violent person.

I don't say anything. Because the fact is, my dad was the king of making up stories like the sand fairy. He'd take any everyday thing and spin such a web of hilarity that we'd hang on every word. When I was little, I used to sit in the bathtub, waterlogged and pruney, while he perched on the toilet and told story after story about the creatures who lived in my toes, or the bath mermaids who needed shampoo to surf. And my mom would lean against the doorframe and listen and laugh, and everything seemed as safe and happy and right as the world could possibly seem.

And this summer, when it was the first time I was together with all my cousins without him, I tried to tell a story the way he would. But the words felt thick and stupid in my mouth. And Daniel, my youngest cousin, looked up at me, disappointed, before asking, "Where's Uncle Tomo? He tells better stories!" And all the others shushed him, like maybe I hadn't noticed that my dad wasn't there.

By the time we're done discussing Alice's random octopus story, I'm fine. I mean, it's not like I spend time reliving the misery of my perfectly nice parents getting a perfectly normal divorce.

I roll my eyes and sit back down, propping my Chuck

Taylors on one of the stools. (Rule Violation #4, obviously. They're bum drums, not footstools, according to Ms. Davis. The sound you hear is the sound of every student here trying not to gag.)

"Yeah. Alice, it sounds like you should meet my cousins. They'd love you," I say, and I'm relieved my voice sounds like it should, not like a mildly hysterical toddler hyena, which was my fear.

"I think this is a really interesting discussion, because it leads into something else: Is it ever okay to lie to make someone feel better?" Ms. Lewiston asks.

"Yes, and can I have my Starburst?" I ask, relieved that the conversation is moving away from me.

But Ms. Lewiston shakes her head. "Yours is on probation. That wasn't really a lie." She holds up her hand to stop what is about to be my impassioned protest.

"Don't mess with a messer, Theo. The goal here is to open up. To be brave and a little vulnerable. To say something that you're not totally sure how other people will react to. Think about it. We'll come back to you."

She looks at my face and smiles.

I don't smile back. I look at her and, remembering her confession on the floor yesterday, think about lorikeets, those horrible screechy parrots that I once fed at a zoo.

Before I can say anything, though, Erik interrupts. "I

think it's totally okay to lie sometimes. I mean, you have to. Like, for politeness or whatever."

"We call that a social contract," Ms. Lewiston says. "Right. But when? How can you tell if you're lying to be nice or to save your own skin?"

Erik opens his mouth, then closes it again. After a second, Ms. Lewiston turns. "Andre? What about you?"

Andre looks a little taken aback, but within a second he's managed his half-lidded mellow look again. "Yeah, I mean, it's a slippery slope, I guess," he says. "You tell someone their music sounds dope, and that's just being nice. But then they want to jam with you, or they ask you to listen to their demo tape, or whatever, and you're stuck." He looks down. "I mean, nobody wants to hurt someone's feelings. Or make enemies. But sometimes if you lie, it snowballs."

I stare at him, my head cocked. That's probably the most I've ever heard him say.

"So even a well-intentioned lie can backfire, right?" Ms. Lewiston says. "Can anyone think of a time they lied and it was the right choice? They're glad they did it?"

I think about my mom asking me if I could bear it if we sold our house, the one with my loft bed and the giant beech tree in the backyard. I knew it was stupid to keep such a huge place for the two of us. And I knew that if I said no, that I *couldn't* bear it, we'd find a way to stay. But I lied. I told her I'd think about it. And I cried like a freaking baby into my pillow all night. And most of the next night. And then I practiced the Jedi stuff I used to be totally into and kept my voice level and relaxed and told her it was fine, that it was just a house. And I'm glad I did.

My eyes meet Molly's, and I almost gasp at how . . . *wrecked* . . . she looks. Whatever lie she's thinking about, it's a big one.

CHAPTER 10

Discussing Stories, Which Sounds Chill but Totally Isn't Once

Sock Puppets Are Involved

We keep talking about lies, which is sort of depressing. But Ms. Lewiston keeps flinging Starbursts at us, so it's livelier than it sounds. Making it even more exciting is that her aim is pretty terrible, and at one point she sends an orange one flying all the way over Andre's head, past Biography, and into Historical Fiction. Mayhem ensues as we all scramble for it, and in the scuffle, the nail falls out of Alice's hand.

After that Ms. Lewiston announces it's time for us to return to the classroom for lunch.

When we get there, she claps her hands. "While you eat, you're going to read a story about some kids, not that different from you all, who participated in a Restorative

Justice Circle. Then when you're done, I'll be putting you into pairs and you'll act out some of what you think is happening. Sound good?"

I think this sounds like literally the worst idea in the entire history of bad ideas, but I don't say anything. Molly sighs so loudly they can hear it in New Hampshire, and her This Is So Stupid I Want to Stab Someone face pretty much says it all. Meanwhile, Erik's pulling dead skin off a scab on his elbow, Alice is reapplying the fake nail, and Andre appears to be communing with something outside the window.

It's going to be a long afternoon.

Ms. Lewiston looks around and smiles like that was exactly the response she was hoping for. Once she finishes handing out the story, she heads back to Erik, giving him an old-school tape player and headphones. Erik takes it and puts it on his desk without ever looking up.

Interesting.

Ms. Lewiston stands again. "Okay, so enjoy."

We must all look a little skeptical, because she does that spectacular one-eyebrow raise. "And who knows? Maybe I'll have more rewards."

With that she's out the door.

With a dramatic sigh, Molly shakes the photocopied

sheets, rustling them as loudly as it's possible to rustle paper, and starts to read.

The story's pretty interesting, I guess. It's about this kid who's what my mom would call a real piece of work . . . nasty and mean and a seriously violent bully. He beats people up, usually without a good reason, and then one time he beats up a kid so badly that the kid gets a major concussion and has to drop out of school because of panic attacks and stuff. But then we find out more, like that the bully kid was abused and had a really brutal home life. But that doesn't make him any less of a nightmare. So basically the bully kid gets sent to a foster home, and the foster parents are into this restorative justice thing. And they ask the cops—because the concussion kid's parents are pressing charges—if the other family and the police would be willing to participate in a restorative justice process. So then they all—the victim, his parents, the police, the kid who did it, his foster parents, and even the teacher and a bunch of kids at the school who witnessed it—get together and talk about it.

The story's only around ten pages long, but it takes place over a year, or maybe even longer. The first time they circle up, they do the same thing we do with the whole candle and talking stick, but the victim kid is so scared and nervous that he actually pees himself. It's humiliating even reading this, and I get mad at Ms. Lewiston for making us do it. I mean, does she think that's going to happen to me? It's not like anyone beat me to a pulp.

Anyway, it goes from there, and the various people talk about how it affected them. And I don't know, the part that gets to me is when the *teacher,* of all people, breaks down crying so hard he can't talk. Finally he says he was bullied as a kid, and has gotten into martial arts since then and has never felt threatened again, but that the day this kid got beaten up he was out of the room on a personal call, and he felt like it was all his fault, like he was as useless and weak as he'd ever been. He apologizes to the kid who got beat up, asking him to forgive him, and meanwhile the bully is watching, trying to understand all the ways his actions messed everyone up.

I read faster, wanting to know how this ends, if there's ever a way that everyone can forgive him. Amazingly, they *do,* though it takes a LOT of these circles before they finally get there. I'm talking most of a year. I'm exhausted just reading about it.

And the LAST thing I want to do is act it out. I stare out the window and hope Ms. Lewiston gets a medically unique case of amnesia where she remembers her name and family and everything but forgets that she had a jaw-droppingly awful plan to make us pair up and do awkward emo improv games.

Sadly, when she comes in a few minutes later, that hasn't happened. She has us all stand up and close our eyes.

"Okay, keep your eyes closed and think about a character from the story you want to take on. There's the victim and the perpetrator, of course, but also think about the others. Were they bystanders who did nothing? Or upstanders who tried to take action? How would they be feeling? There's no right or wrong answer, and if two partners want to be the same character, well, that's okay too. You can act out how she or he might be feeling inside."

Her voice comes closer, and I squint out of my closed eyes. Across from me, I see Molly doing the same thing, but she scowls and squeezes her eyes tight when she sees me.

"I'm going to take your hand and gently lead you over to your partner, joining you two together," Lewiston continues.

My shoulders tense up, and I brace myself. I swear, if I had known emo improv was part of the Justice Circle, I would *not* have agreed to do it.

But she takes my hand, and I try not to jerk it away from her, and next thing I know I'm holding what can only be the size-XXL, sweaty, basketball-wielding hand of Erik, Total Suspect #1.

Freaking PERFECT.

I drop his hand like it's covered in dog poop and open my eyes.

Molly's standing next to Jax, her face aflame with her How Can the World Be This Stupid look. In fairness, Jax doesn't look a whole lot happier. He's slouched over, his hat almost covering his eyes. On the other side of the room Alice and Andre stand next to each other. I notice after a second that Alice is clutching Andre's sleeve, and her eyes are still closed. Andre looks a little pained.

Ms. Lewiston, on the other hand, looks like this is part of the plan, which makes me question her sanity. "Now!" she says, her voice far too upbeat. "Let's do this. But before we get into character, can we start by talking about the difference between restorative justice and punitive justice?" She looks around. "Who wants to begin?"

Molly snorts. "Well, punitive means that whoever broke the rule gets punished. Like, in this case, only the person who actually ruined Theo's photos would be in trouble." She glares around, as though to say that punitive justice would be fine by her.

"That's true, Molly," Ms. Lewiston says. "And what are some reasons that restorative justice is different?"

Andre speaks up, gently shaking his arm until Alice lets go. "In restorative justice it's all about what happened before, and what has to happen to make things right. It's not all about the victim, or even the . . . you know, perpetrator. Like in the story, Derek's the guy who did it, but he's not really who the story's about."

Ms. Lewiston nods. "Exactly. That's exactly right. The story is about all the people affected by Derek's actions. So feel free, in this exercise, to tap into whoever you want. Really think about what's going on in that person's mind." She smiles. "Who wants to start?"

Jax stares at her for a second, then bends down, kicks off his shoe, and pulls off a sock, placing it over his hand. "Yo, if it's okay with you, I'm going to perform my character through this sock puppet."

Molly moves back a few steps. "Put. That. ON," she says, crossing her arms across her chest.

Jax just shakes his head and balances on one sneaker, his other bony bare foot dangling off the floor. "Nope. This is my . . . you know, instrument. Tell you what, I'll be Jamal, the kid who got beat up." He turns to Molly and makes the sock puppet talk. "Who you want to be?"

Molly looks like she wants to be anyone in the world who isn't in this room, but after a second she sighs and says that she'll be Jamal's friend, Alicia.

"When you're ready," Ms. Lewiston says softly.

There's a pause. Then Jax begins.

"AHHHHHHHHHHHHH!" he screams so loudly that Alice jumps a full foot into the air. "I BEEN BEATEN REALLY BAD!!! I'M NEARLY DEAD!!!!!!!!! HELLLLLLLLLLLLLP!!!" He waves his hand around, the white sock flapping wildly.

I cover my ears.

Ms. Lewiston raises her hands. She has to call his name a few times before he can hear her over his shouting.

"Jax. JAX! Hey! Wow! That's some great emotion, but let's pick up where the individuals are *in* the Justice Circle. Okay? Not at the time of the incident."

Jax pauses mid-scream. "Oh. Okay. My bad."

Slowly I lower my hands.

Ms. Lewiston looks a little rattled. "I tell you what, why don't you take a minute to think about it, and we'll have Andre and Alice give it a try, okay?"

Alice claps her hands. "Oh, excellent. Andre, I'll be Derek, the guy who did it, okay? What about you?"

Andre shrugs. "I don't know. Maybe Mr. Sauk, the teacher."

"Great," Ms. Lewiston says. "Take it away."

Andre looks deeply unsure, but he gives it a try. "Uh. Yo, Derek. I'm glad we have a chance to talk with you about what went down. As your teacher, I feel really guilty, because I should have protected the other students. And I wish I hadn't left the room, because—"

Before Andre can say anything more, Alice is pacing away from him, her face twisted and wild.

"My temper! My accursed temper will RUIN ME! And maybe that would be a good thing! Maybe the world would be better without me, but what of all the others who I've ruined in my path? How can there possibly be redemption? THEIR SPIRITS WILL HAUNT ME TO MY DEATH AND BEYOND!" She tears at her hair in apparent anguish.

Andre's mouth drops open.

Alice continues. "There is so much horror in my past!" She drops to her knees. "Will I ever escape it? ANSWER ME, CRUEL FATES!"

Silence.

Then she stage-whispers to Andre, *"Now you say something."*

Andre coughs, then says, feebly, "Well, you know, Derek, I was . . . uh . . . I was bullied as a kid, so it was really hard for me to accept the fact that, as an adult, I wasn't there to help Jamal. Like, I felt powerless again, even though you didn't hurt me directly."

"LET ME ATTEMPT MY PENANCE!!" Alice shrieks, flailing onto her back. The fake nail goes flying.

Andre steps back in alarm, and Ms. Lewiston waves her hands a few times to get their attention. She looks a little desperate, and I'd feel bad if it weren't for the fact that (1) I kind of LOVE Alice's Shakespearean version of Derek, and (2) I suspect it's me and Erik up next.

"Wow. Wow, Alice, that was some great intensity," Ms. Lewiston says. "Can you tell us what you were thinking?"

Alice sits up and beams. "Thank you! I guess I wanted to show how horrible Derek would feel, once he really understood the damage he had done. Like, in a way it's a worse punishment than going to reform school or whatever."

"That's wonderful," Ms. Lewiston starts, but Alice interrupts.

"And in the next scene, I was thinking that his getting forgiveness was like, I don't know, like all his toxic poison was being drained out of him. Like he's being *purged*. Here, I'll show you!" She leaps to her feet.

Ms. Lewiston puts up her hand. "I'm sure that would be amazing, Alice, but let's let Erik and Theo have a turn, okay?"

I shoot her a dirty look. I would *so much* rather watch Alice purge herself of toxic hate. Erik looms next to me like a polyester-upholstered tree. He puts an arm around my shoulders and I flinch away.

"Who do you want to be?" he asks. "I was thinking I'd try Jamal."

I roll my eyes. What a subtle way to deflect suspicion. "Fine. I'll be Derek."

Ms. Lewiston nods. "Whenever you're ready."

We're both silent, then both start talking at once. Erik turns red. "Sorry! Go ahead."

"No, you go."

"No, you."

More silence.

This is possibly the most painful thing I have ever done, and that includes getting nine vaccinations at once when I was eleven.

"FINE." I stare at Erik. "Look, Jamal," I say, sounding like someone nailing the audition for the stupidest actor in the world. "I can't change anything that happened, so I don't really know what you want from me. I screwed up. Badly. But now it's over, so I don't really know why I'm here. I mean, I'm sorry. I'm really, really sorry. But what else can I say?"

Erik looks straight ahead, right past me. "I . . . I don't want to talk to Derek. I get that we're here to make things better, but I can't look at him. It brings back all the scary feelings. I want to forgive him, but I don't know how. Everything is so hard now. I cry at night—"

"Okay, we're done!" I'm halfway across the room. I don't need to hear Erik's sniveling version of the sad beat-up kid. Is that who he thinks I am? My stomach churns. I'm out. This is so freaking stupid.

"I need to go to the bathroom. Sorry." I make for the door, and the last thing I hear before it slams is Ms. Lewiston calling my name. But I don't even slow down.

In the bathroom I take a few deep breaths, then splash water on my face. I know I need to go back, and fast, before (1) Ms. Lewiston sends someone in to make sure my poor fragile self isn't weeping into the urinals, or (2) Erik comes along to see just how pathetic I really am. I close my eyes for a second, then open them, shaking my neck and shoulders until I don't look like a hunted animal. When I'm sure I look normal, I head back.

I can hear the group before I even get to the doorway. It doesn't sound good. Carefully I open the door and peer in. Molly, Erik, and Jax, who's still wearing the sock on his hand like a puppet, are grouped in the middle of the room.

Jax is yelling, his sock-puppet mouth opening and closing. It looks like he found a pen and added eyes while I was gone. He's still channeling Jamal. "Why would you do what you did to me? That's the real question: WHY? Why would you want to hurt people? What did I ever do to you?"

Meanwhile, Molly, who has apparently taken on the role of Derek, is standing red-faced and angry next to him. "I . . ." She pauses. "This is so dumb!" she says finally. "I have no idea why someone would—"

"Just do your best, Molly," Ms. Lewiston says quietly. "Think about what someone might have been feeling, to be so violent."

Molly stays silent.

Erik steps forward. "Uh. I'm Derek's friend . . . you know, one of the guys he used to hang out with when he was doing all his crazy stuff." He gulps. "Well, I just want to say that, um, Derek, you were a friend of mine, we were like a team, you know. But, um, now we're not friends. I can't . . . You can't do stuff like you did, man. And it's not because you got busted. But I can't handle how crazy you get, you know?"

I sigh, loudly. Erik should definitely not pursue a career in acting. Molly just scowls harder, then finally speaks.

"I can't . . . I couldn't help it," she says, her voice barely above a whisper. "Everything hurt so bad, and nothing made it better. Nothing but hurting other people."

There's silence for a second, then Jax's sock puppet

opens its mouth. "EXCEPT FOR STEALING CHOCO-LATE!"

Molly freezes, mouth open. "WHAT?" She lurches forward, whips the sock off his hand, and flings it at his face.

Jax catches it but loses his balance and staggers into Erik. "It was just a jo—"

"YOU—YOU ARE SUCH A—"

"CHILL OUT!"

"I CAN'T BELIEVE—"

A piercing whistle cuts through their shouting, and they both go silent. Ms. Lewiston has two fingers in her mouth.

"Enough. Both of you. Jax, I understand you thought you were making a joke. But this isn't the time."

Jax stands there, clutching his sock to his chest. He scowls. Nods.

Ms. Lewiston goes on. "You all shared different elements of what makes this so powerful and so hard. Going through something traumatic like they do in the story can bond people together. Or it can tear them apart. Which is why restorative justice is so important. It's all about finding a way forward."

She sighs. "It may be that we need to get to know each other a little better before we dig in on this. It's hard work, what I'm asking you to do."

I nod along with everyone else, but part of me wonders:

If this is going to work, do I need to be more traumatized? Because I'm committed to this process. Seriously, I am. I get how it's better for everyone if we move forward and get some answers and figure out how to "deal with it as a community" or whatever, but nobody hurt me. I mean, there was poor Jamal with broken ribs and a concussion and serious trauma like after a war. Part of me feels like a big fake even being here, with my poor boo-hoo-Theo's-photos-are-messed-up life. But I don't dare say that to Ms. Lewiston. For her sake, I'll pretend this all really matters.

CHAPTER 11

I Think Death Metal Is the Huge Revelation of the Day, Until I Get to Death

We all go take a bathroom break, and when we get back, everyone's calmed down. Jax apologizes again for disrespecting Molly's process and using a sock puppet, and Alice asks why the sock puppet was the problem, because she really liked that part, and Erik says he thought Alice's version of Derek was really cool, and I'm left once again wondering why on earth I'm here.

The more time we all spend together, the less I understand what happened. It's like some cosmic joke: the more we talk, the worse I feel. I'm pretty sure that Erik must have done it, but is he really able to fake looking so clueless? And how much do the others know? I mean, someone must have seen something, right? I don't know. I don't know anything.

Ms. Lewiston claps her hands, and I head over to rejoin the circle.

"It may have been a little premature to work through the story like that. It was a lot to ask of you, and I appreciate the effort. But now I want to switch gears a little, and get to know each other a little better. I want to talk about something that matters to each of us, something that maybe isn't schoolwork—"

Here Molly looks disappointed.

"—but that we are intrinsically motived to work on."

She turns to Jax. "And we're going to start with you."

Jax looks startled, his usual I-got-this grin absent from his face.

"I ... uh. I'm *intrinsically motivated* to chillax, you know?" he starts, but Ms. Lewiston has a hand up before he can finish.

"Nope. We're dropping the act, for a little while. I need you to take this seriously. There is, I promise you, no wrong answer. If it's something dangerous or illegal, I'll have to talk with you about it, and, yes, reach out to your parents if I'm really concerned. But otherwise"—she waves her arms—"the sky's the limit."

Jax is silent for a second. Then he leans back and spreads his legs wide, sliding down in the chair. "Okay, cool," he says. "I guess, I'm pretty into hip-hop. Like, I love listening to new songs, waiting for new mixtapes to drop, stuff like that." He pauses. "But that's probably not even what you mean, because it's not like I'm recording or anything, I just—"

Ms. Lewiston interrupts him again, but gently this time. "That's totally fine. Tell us more. Who are some of your favorite artists?"

Jax leans forward, uncrossing his arms. "Okay, so this is controversial, I know, but I'm always going to defend Wu-Tang Clan, because of the sheer volume of amazing artists in that group. And while I like Kendrick Lamar okay, and I won't say anything negative against Kanye, I don't think he's even close to proving himself the way Wu Tang has."

He goes on, like someone turned a faucet. "And I know there's a lot of stereotyping of rap for being violent and misogynist and stuff—"

He pauses again. "That means sexist against women," he says, looking around.

Molly gets her Everything Is a Total Outrage face on. "I *know* what it means! And rap has that reputation because it's TRUE!"

Ms. Lewiston holds up a hand. "Hold up, Molly. Jax, thank you for defining the word. It's an important one, and not everyone knows it." She looks around.

Erik shrugs and nods. "Yeah, dude. No idea. Would have thought it was some kind of scientist. You know, biologist, misogynist . . . ?"

We all kind of snort-laugh at that, even Molly, who mutters, "Well, if so, there are a whole bunch of schools giving out *that* degree."

Ms. Lewiston goes on. "But we'll save that conversation for now. Jax, go on. You were saying you think rap gets stereotyped."

Jax nods. "It does. I mean, yeah, there are a bunch of cra— I mean, bad songs, but come on. Check out some others. Listen to T.I. or Common or K'naan. These brothers are speaking truth."

He looks around like he's daring us to disagree, but no one says anything.

"And you know, it suc— I mean, it really makes me mad when people judge it without even knowing. And then judge *me* for liking it."

I consider this. I guess I did probably think most rap was all about bling and expensive cars and partying. Would I have an opinion of someone who listens only to hip-hop? If I'm being honest, probably. Judging people is pretty much my favorite in-school pastime.

I remember Jax sneering at us for ogling his lunch and wonder, for the first time, what it's like being black in

Shipton. I guess most people at school listen to Top Forty, or the kind of indie rock that my dad used to call happy-mopey-camping music. I look at Jax and get a crash of sympathy. I mean, food-chain-wise, he's not like me or Andre, or even Alice. He's got friends and plays a bunch of sports and is pretty popular. He's predator, not prey.

But still.

"Anyway," he winds down. "That's something I care about."

"Thanks, Jax," Ms. Lewiston says. "I'm glad to know that."

She looks around. "Anyone want to comment?"

Continuing the trend of shocking me with unexpected behaviors, Andre raises his hand. "Yeah. I'm curious. Do your friends and family like the same music you do?"

Ms. Lewiston smiles at Andre like he just told her they're long-lost cousins. "That's a great question. Jax?"

Jax leans back again and kicks his high-tops out in front of him. "My friends do. That's probably most of what we have in common and pretty much what we talk about." He gives a short not-funny laugh. "But my family . . . yeah. Have you met my family?"

We all do the kind of nod/head-shake/shrug thing that is as noncommittal as humanly possible without imitating a corpse. Jax is adopted, and has a bunch of brothers and two white dads. I remember them from Family Nights in elementary school, when they were always the loudest people there. But . . . in a good way. One of his dads always wore awesome T-shirts, like "You're Entitled to Your Own Opinion, But Not Your Own Facts" or "Kill Your Television."

Jax does his not-funny laugh again. "They know nothing. My parents try to read up and stuff, but it's embarrassing."

He goes on. "Kwame's dad . . . he's, like, an expert. He grew up with Grandmaster Flash and LL Cool J, and he's like . . . like a professor of rap, practically." He shrugs. "But not in my family."

Ms. Lewiston nods. "That can be hard sometimes," she says.

Jax doesn't answer, but his expression seems to agree.

There's a moment of silence; then Andre speaks again. My eyebrows shoot up. Two unsolicited statements from Andre! Unusual things are afoot.

"Yeah, I . . . uh . . . I don't really listen to rap, but my older brother and sister do, and they think my music is weak. So I know what you mean, I guess."

Jax looks over at him, skeptical. "What kind of stuff do you listen to? Like, classical or jazz or something?"

"Naw. I kind of . . . well, I play drums. In a death metal group. We're . . . we actually play gigs and stuff."

It should be noted that if I had five hundred guesses as to what Andre does with his spare time, death metal drumming would have been number one billion. Maybe two billion.

We all stare at him. Andre stares determinedly at his desk like there's a secret code there needed to unlock the bomb shelter before we all blow up.

Finally Jax speaks, and I think it's fair to say he pretty much says what the rest of us are thinking. Well, except Alice, who hasn't seemed to notice the conversation but is slowly drawing an intricate spiderweb on her hand in black Sharpie.

"You're *kidding*. Right? You're messing with us? Death metal? Like big-haired white dudes thrashing away in leather pants?" He shakes his head, looking baffled. "That's angry white boy music."

Andre looks up. "Actually, no. That's not all it is. At all."

Molly asks, "What do you mean you play gigs? Like, people pay you?"

Andre nods. "Our band is . . . um . . . getting pretty well-known."

Molly looks impatient. "What band? And what do you mean? Do you play around here?"

"Our band is Skeleton Curse, and we play. Um. Well,

Boston. And New York, this past summer. We have a . . . uh . . . YouTube channel. With a bunch of followers. Like, fifty thousand. Ish." Andre looks down.

He mumbles this last thing, so we all lean forward trying to hear him. When I compute what he's saying, I lean back.

Flummoxed was a vocab word last month, meaning totally taken by surprise or caught off guard. And I guess I'd say we're all looking pretty flummoxed by Andre's revelation.

Molly looks at me, and I shrug; then she looks at Alice. Erik looks at Jax, who looks at Ms. Lewiston, who is *not* looking surprised. Which is even more flummoxing, if that's possible.

"Did you know about Andre's band?" I ask her.

"Sure. He's something of a celebrity. Not my kind of music, but it's pretty amazing, what he can do on those drums," she says.

Andre goes back to code breaking his desk.

Erik shakes his head slowly. "I had no idea," he says, his voice as baffled as the kid who just found out there's no Easter Bunny. "You'd never know it from . . . well, you know."

While I hate to agree with Erik "I might force you to eat

your gym sock" Estrale, I do know. Andre is phytoplank-ton, remember? How can you go to school with someone for years and not know this giant thing about him?

Andre shrugs. "Anyway, I mean . . . I just wanted to say I know what it's like when family and friends don't always get your music," he says to Jax.

Jax nods slowly. "Yeah, I guess," he says. "Yo, what's your band's name again? I'll look you up when I get home."

"Me too!" This is from Alice, who's looked up from her doodling, her eyes flicking back and forth from Jax to Andre. "Maybe I can use some of your music in one of my films! With full credit, obvs."

Andre actually smiles at her, a big, real smile, that shows his braces. "Horror movies are totally dope," he says. "It'd be sick to be in one."

Alice's eyes go huge and wide. "We could *totally* make a slasher movie where the band's being hunted! Oh! It would be so good!" She shakes her head so that the nail wobbles, and she smiles, a rather frightening smile, honestly. "I can picture the blood splattering the white drum set."

We respectfully stay silent for a moment, allowing them their vision, but then Molly breaks it.

"You guys are *so* weird," she says, but her voice is more Isn't This Interesting than Get Me a Hazmat Suit, so I think she means it nicely. Maybe.

"That's a great idea," Ms. Lewiston says. "And I hope you'll keep us all posted about the film. But to circle back, let's think about what we've heard. Jax loves rap and doesn't always feel like his family understands or respects it. Andre plays death metal, and *his* family doesn't really get why that's his choice of music. He loves horror movies and would love to be a part of Alice's next filmmaking project." She pauses. "Did any of you know any of this before?"

We all shake our heads.

"How long have you known each other?"

Alice starts counting out loud, starting with kindergarten and then trying to remember if we were all in the same class in fifth grade.

"Approximately, Alice," Ms. Lewiston says.

I think. Six years? Seven?

"We're going to take a stretch break, but I want you all to think about that for a minute." She looks around at each of us. "Do you remember what I wrote on the board the first day?" She points back at the whiteboard.

Be kind, for everyone is fighting unseen battles.

"There's a lot we don't know about each other. Keep that in mind." With that, she pushes back her chair and heads toward the door.

I stay in my seat, listening to the buzz of voices all around me. Erik is regaling Jax with some story about a guy on the basketball team who writes raps and performs them at spoken-word-poetry jams in Boston. Alice and Andre have their heads together, peeping at Alice's notebook, where she's madly scribbling. I look at Molly, who looks as flummoxed as I feel.

"I wasn't expecting that," I say, then brace myself for a classic Molly Why Do You Even Exist response.

But she shakes her head a little, looking far away. "Yeah. Me neither. My . . . I used to know someone who loved death metal, and I've actually heard of Andre's band. They're a big deal."

Her face has gone into that The Curse Has Come Upon Me look again, and I wonder. I wonder lots of things:

1) Who listens to death metal in Molly Claremont's world?
2) Why does she have that Lady of Shalott look?
3) What else don't I know about Molly, or, for that matter, everyone else in this school?

I blame it on the fact this whole thing is so weird, but I blurt out: "Why do you look so sad?"

As soon as I say it, I mentally punch myself in the face a few times. Nothing good is going to come from this. Either she'll tell me and I'll be embroiled in whatever drama

Molly has, thereby breaking that time-honored and oh-so-vital-to-my-survival "stay out of everyone's business" rule. Or she won't, and she'll huff off in a grand flounce, and it will be even more awkward in this room than it already is.

But she turns to me, and her face is so pale her freckles look like someone drew them on.

"My brother died this summer. He was seventeen. He has . . . had . . . um . . ."

She stops talking.

Holy. Crap.

It should be noted that if I thought I felt bad before, I now know that I felt like unicorns and baby pandas compared with how I feel now.

What I want to say is something kind and thoughtful and careful.

What my brain is saying is HOLY CRAP DEAD DEAD DEAD BROTHER DEAD.

What comes out of my mouth is glargbebaggasucksbargle.

It would be spectacular if Alice's zombies wanted to show up Right. About. Now.

But Molly doesn't notice, or is nice enough to pretend not to. So I fake sneeze (which I can do quite well, so that was okay). Then I try again.

"That's awful. I mean, I'm so sorry." I wince. This is

better, but barely. "I don't mean sorry because I did it. Obviously, I didn't have anything to do with it. But I—"

Molly is nicer than I ever gave her credit for. Because instead of shooting me with a How Did You Stay Alive This Long if You're This Stupid look, which I definitely deserve, she smiles, though it's kind of exhausted-looking.

"It's fine. I know what you mean. There's no good thing to say."

I shrug-nod because she's right, but still. Just because there's nothing good to say doesn't mean I have to say something quite so painfully stupid. "Still, it's not fine. I mean, it must be really awful," I goat-bleat.

Wonderful, Theo. Remind her how terrible her life is. I give myself another mental punch, this time somewhere more painful than my face.

But she nods. "Yeah. It *is* really awful. He was sick since he was born, so my parents knew he wouldn't grow, uh"— her voice breaks a little, and she coughs—"up. But, you know."

"Knowing it doesn't make it easier, I don't think," I say. "There's knowing something and there's really getting your brain to believe it."

I think about my dad packing up his stuff. I think about him explaining that he's leaving, that he's moving to Guatemala, that he'll call and Skype and we'll still talk all the time. I understood it at the time: him looking me in the eye and telling me again and again how much he loves me. I nodded to all of this, because I understood each word and concept. But I didn't really understand what it would feel like to look at the empty bookshelves, the pale spot on the floor where his armchair had been, the huge space in the living room where his desk used to sit. "Even when you know something is coming, it doesn't make it any less awful when it happens. You still have to live with it every single day."

Molly looks at me. "Yeah," she says. And though her eyes and the tip of her nose are pink and cry-y, she sounds okay. "Exactly. That's exactly it."

That's all she says, but it should be noted that something about her voice makes up for my earlier nuclear meltdown of conversational skills, and I don't need to mentally punch myself anywhere for the rest of the day. And that day, when we wrap up, I think that maybe I won't have to gnaw my leg off after all.

CHAPTER 12

Ms. Davis Manages to Be So Awful That Even Justice Circle Seems Attractive

The next morning I'm weirdly nervous. Like, almost excited nervous, but the very idea of being excited to go back to Interrogation Room 201 is so unacceptable that I'm annoyed with myself. I wonder if it's possible to get Stockholm syndrome, where captives start to feel all warm and fuzzy toward their jailers, in two days. I yo-yo back and forth between being kind of psyched to see everyone and being annoyed that I even care, and by the time my mom drops me off, I'm sullen and rude to her, and honestly I want to slap myself across the face repeatedly. Possibly with a dead fish or one of Erik's sweat socks or something else unspeakable. I'm a mess.

"Well. I can understand that this whole thing is taking its toll on you," my mom says when she pulls up at the school. "But try to remember I'm on your side."

I don't answer right away and don't open the car door. I realize my mom's going to be late if I don't move. But I stay put. It's like there's Velcro on my butt, holding it to the seat.

My mom rustles for something in her purse, then looks up. Whatever she sees makes her face change.

"Is it really bad?" she asks, her voice quiet in the car.

I shake my head. On the list of things I try not to do, sending my mom into worried-about-Theo mode is right up there at the top, along with pooping at school and getting stuck talking to Mr. "History Is All Around You" Monterro between classes, which *always* results in a tardy slip, no matter how you explain that it wasn't exactly your choice.

Anyway. It's not that my mom's that over-the-top on the parental fussing scale, because she's not. But I guess I never realized, until my dad was gone, that having two parents around was somehow half the stress of having one. The math doesn't make sense, I know, but whatever. Now that it's only me and my mom, I don't want to go there unless I really need to. And this . . . this stupid photography fiasco is hardly worth the drama.

She's still looking at me, so I answer. "It's not that it's awful. I just . . . Why?" I pause. "I mean, I still figure it was Erik Estrale, since his friends are total jerks. How many times has he stood there laughing while his turd-button friends torture some poor nerdlet? But the past two days . . . he's, I don't know. Not that bad. He seems decent. And if he's decent . . . I just don't get why he would do something like this." To my total horror, my voice cracks a little on the last words.

"Are you crying?" Her voice has gone to mama-grizzly-on-attack.

"No." And I'm not. But my face feels hot and stupid. I try to snort in the snot and blink hard.

"You ARE! Sweetie, you are! Oh, Theo. My sweet boy."

Oh. My. God. She's in a full-blown mom hurricane, and I need to get out of here.

"I'm fine. Mom, I swear. I have to go. Loveyoubye." I throw myself out of the car and close the door fast behind me.

The window rolls down immediately.

"You're sure. You're sure you want to do this?" she asks. "Because I'll tell you right now, if you don't, we—"

I pretend I don't hear her and wave goodbye. Alice's gold Lexus has pulled up behind our car, and Alice is climbing out of the passenger side. She appears to be wearing a bathrobe, but a kind of chic, dressy one. Or maybe it's a dress meant to look like a robe. Who knows? I look back at my mom.

"Mom. I'm fine. All good, I swear." I wave one last time and turn away.

She starts to answer, but whoever's driving Alice's car taps the horn once, then leans on it. As I glance back, I see my mom waving wildly out the window before driving off.

Perfect.

I look at Alice. She looks back at me, blinking. Well, two of her eyes are blinking. She has a third one installed in the middle of her forehead, but that one doesn't seem to blink.

She says: "Sorry my dad is so impatient."

I nod. "Sorry my mom gave him the finger."

She shrugs. Together we walk into the school for day three.

When we get to the room, Ms. Lewiston hands me a cup. "Yesterday was like trying to eat a fine meal with Oliver Twist outside the window, pressing his nose against the glass. Here."

I am so absurdly grateful I almost cry for real. The smell of fairies and springtime and magic wafts out of the cup, and I close my eyes and inhale.

"It's half-decaf," she warns.

I shrug. "That'll work." I take another deep breath. "Thank you. Seriously."

"You're seriously welcome," she says. Then, stepping closer, she asks, "How are you doing? I know this has to be hard on you, but—"

I interrupt. "It's fine. I'm glad we're ... you know. Restoring justice and all that. I'm good."

She looks like she wants to say more, but I avoid eye contact, staring at the coffee like it might bolt if I don't stay alert.

"Do you think everyone else is doing okay?" she asks. "As we talked about yesterday, this incident affects everyone here in different ways."

I glance around the room. Molly and Alice are sitting closer together, and Alice seems to be explaining in great detail how she got the eyeball in the middle of her forehead. Andre looks like he's listening too, and on the other side of the room Jax and Erik have their heads bent over an issue of *Sportsballs and Sweaty Things* (possibly not the actual title) and are murmuring things like "Curry is the bomb" and "LeBron, though ... Beast" and interrupting each other so constantly I doubt they're even listening. I get a kind of cold, empty feeling.

"Sure," I say, and my voice sounds flat, even to me. "I think they're fine."

Before we even get ourselves into our circle, the door opens and Ms. Davis storms in. She's in her usual work-type suit, but her hair is a hot mess of frizz and she's not wearing her usual orange-tinted face makeup and dried-blood-colored lipstick. She looks, honestly, like someone who was happily enjoying vacation week but then had to come in to school. You and me both, buttercup.

She stomps over to Ms. Lewiston.

"Can we speak privately? NOW?"

Ms. Lewiston sighs, so quietly we can barely hear it. "Of course," she says, and the two of them walk out.

Needless to say, we all remain totally silent, eavesdropping like it's our job. Not that it's hard; Davis is *not* using her inside voice.

"Were you in the library? Why were you in the library? You realize it's vacation week and we have limited custodial services, not to mention limited funds for heat and electric?"

"Yes, Kristina, we were in the library. I discussed it with Ms. Cody—"

"Ms. Cody is not the principal of the school! I am, at least for now, and I was called—at home!—by Roy Saunders, who wanted to make sure he was authorized to take the extra time to clean in there. I had given him strict orders to stay with a very limited schedule this week! Every penny counts! When I asked him why the library needed to be cleaned, he informed me that *you* had told him to turn on the lights and the heat. So I came down to ascertain that this wasn't a mistake, but that you had in fact overridden my orders."

Silence.

Then: "Well?" Davis says.

Ms. Lewiston's voice is polite. "I'm sorry, did you ask a question?"

Jax gives a snort and I hear him whisper, "Oh, *snap*!"

"Yes, I asked a question! I asked if you had overridden my orders!" Ms. Davis barks.

Andre coughs a little. I catch his eye and we both grin, comfortable in the knowledge that there was no question asked. Point for Ms. Lewiston.

But Davis isn't done. "And dare I ask if there are any great revelations from this justice plan of yours? Because I'm afraid they will need to spend some time without you this morning. As I'm already here in school, I will ask that you join me in the office. They can sit silently and read until lunch." Her heels click down the hallway.

After a second the door opens and Ms. Lewiston comes back in. She smiles, but not like she means it. "Kids, Ms. Davis and I need to work on something this morning. There is another restorative justice story that you can read and discuss. I have copies in my bag. Like yesterday, please use this time for fruitful discussion." She pauses. "Or Ms. Davis feels you can use this time for silent reading."

We all nod. While the six of us might not have much in common, or trust each other, for that matter, I think it's fair to say we're 100 percent committed to doing the opposite of whatever Ms. Davis says.

CHAPTER 13

Day Three Assessments

Date: Feb. 20

Name: *Molly Claremont*

What happened and what were you thinking at the time of the incident?

I was really distracted that day. I honestly can't say what I was thinking.

What have you thought about since?

It's been ... weird, hanging out with everyone. I mean, Theo's a nice guy. He's quiet, but he's pretty smart, and his photos are good, and nobody dislikes him, I don't think. So I don't know why they'd do this.

What about this has been hardest for you?
We really need to get some answers. I CANNOT be
suspended. Like, this week at school is bad, but I can
deal with it. But suspension? No way.

**What do you think needs to be done to make things as
right as possible?**
If Theo's okay, then maybe we should just move on.
We can try to make Theo feel better, maybe. But right
now I don't really know.

**Is there anything at all you'd like to share confidentially
with Ms. Lewiston?**
If no one confesses at the end of this, will it all be
over?

Name: Andre Hall

**What happened and what were you thinking at the
time of the incident?**
Nothing new here ... no idea who was even around
the gallery, since, as I said, I wasn't THERE.

What have you thought about since?

I guess I wonder why it takes something bad happening for the six of us to talk to each other. Theo's pretty chill and we have a bunch of classes together, but we're strangers. Tells you something about us, maybe, but something about school, too.

What about this has been hardest for you?

Usually keeping low-key works pretty well for me. But this whole thing, that no one even noticed I was gone (and really, we're not talking about a giant crowd), that stings.

What do you think needs to be done to make things as right as possible?

The more we all hang out and talk, the more I think someone's not being square with us. Because I don't see it. What people are showing doesn't add up to someone messing with Theo. Something's off. All I know is that it wasn't me.

Is there anything at all you'd like to share confidentially with Ms. Lewiston?

You know, Theo keeps acting really chill and like it's not bothering him, but let's have some real talk:

it would seriously mess with my head if someone
hated on me like someone hated on him.

Name: *Erik Estrale*

- -

What happened and what were you thinking at the time of the incident?
Honestly, I just ... I don't know what to think.

What have you thought about since?
*People always blame the jocks, because they think
we're meatheads or idiots or something. But taking
athletics seriously means that you have discipline
and commitment, and yeah, one or two guys are total
jerks, but the rest of us get judged for it. For the
record, I would never EVER ruin Theo's photos. They
were really cool.*

What about this has been hardest for you?
*I really hate that something like sports gets a
bad rap because of a few idiots. Most of us aren't
like that.*

What do you think needs to be done to make things as right as possible?

I don't know what would help. I really don't.

Is there anything at all you'd like to share confidentially with Ms. Lewiston?

What if someone
   Never mind. Forget it.

Name: Alice Shu

What happened and what were you thinking at the time of the incident?

I don't have anything new to add. Sorry.

What have you thought about since?

Reading that story was really interesting. It makes me think about all the people who tease me and take my stuff. I wonder what else is going on with them? Probably a lot.

What about this has been hardest for you?

Nothing, really. I don't mind being here.

What do you think needs to be done to make things as right as possible?

If someone told the truth, do you think they'd be forgiven? Hard to know, really.

Is there anything at all you'd like to share confidentially with Ms. Lewiston?

I wonder if anyone would be willing to tell something if they could tell it anonymously. Just wondering.

Name: Jax Fletcher

What happened and what were you thinking at the time of the incident?

I want to help out, but I have nothing to offer.

What have you thought about since?

You know, the darkroom thing might have been a mistake. But the gallery? That was some nasty work. And it stinks. Because I seriously don't know why anyone would want to hurt Theo. He's a pretty chill guy.

What about this has been hardest for you?

Sitting around school all week is BRUTAL. But truth? It's not that bad hanging out with the other inmates, I mean Justice Club peeps. They're kind of wack, but in a good way.

What do you think needs to be done to make things as right as possible?

No idea. I don't know that we're getting any closer to answers.

Is there anything at all you'd like to share confidentially with Ms. Lewiston?

I guess ... sometimes people do stupid things totally by accident. It does happen.

CHAPTER 14

Oh, the Places We'll Go
(and the Bad Decisions We'll Make)!

Once Davis and Lewiston leave, I wander around, unsure where to go. Finally I slump in a seat and take a huge restorative sip of coffee.

Erik frowns and shakes his head. "Dude. You know that's, like, poison to your system. You might get a jolt of energy, but it doesn't last. You need something like this." He holds up a half-gallon jug of what looks like nuclear waste. Seriously, it's almost-glowing.

"PowerQuest," he announces proudly. "Replenishes all electrolytes, *and* includes"—he squints at the label—"*acai* berry essence. So."

I look at Jax, then nod thoughtfully, like this is actual science and not corporate repackaging of toxic waste.

"Right," I say, and I try very hard to make sure my voice

is saying "You've got to be kidding me have you ever even researched corporate sugar-water products?" I'm trying so hard to push out all that snark that it comes out as a gargling cough.

Jax looks pained. "Dude. Point that crap away from me."

"Sorry," I choke. "Allergies."

Erik looks smug. "Because you're drinking too much coffee and not enough of this! It has *acai berries*!" He takes a big gulp, and the smell of artificial lemon-scented industrial cleaner comes out of the bottle. I wince.

In addition to the obvious problem of his toxic-waste habit, Erik is stressing out over something, and it's making me seriously nervous. He keeps staring at me, and I can't tell whether it's a Dude I Want to Tell You Something stare or a Dude I Am Planning to Punch You in the Nuts stare. Needless to say, I'm having a low-grade freak-out. I wouldn't put it past him to admit to trashing my stuff when there are no teachers around, then threaten all kinds of hideous payback if I spill. This is why we need adults in the room. . . . It's like having coyotes hang out with a bunch of fluffy bunnies until the zookeepers come back.

I turn my chair away from him and face the opposite wall. I don't want to give him the chance to say anything. I don't want to hear it unless Lewiston is in the room. . . . I'm not counting on anyone here to be a witness if it's his word against mine.

To my relief, Erik-with-the-creepy-stare settles down. Once again he has his earphones on, his size-eleven feet propped up on the chair in front of him. Jax has made a pillow out of his hoodie and is napping on his desk.

After around a half hour Jax groans, stretches, knocks his water bottle off the desk, scaring all of us, and groans again. "Holy. Crap," he mutters, twisting his back and neck and nearly falling out of the chair. "I think I drooled. Dude. That's just nasty."

Molly briefly closes her eyes as though she's in pain.

I can't help it. I catch Andre's eye again and grin.

Jax untangles himself from his chair and stands up, stomping his feet.

"Okay." STOMP. "I'm awake." STOMP. "How is everybody?" STOMP STOMP.

Molly glares icy-cold shards of What Is Wrong with You at him.

"Foot's asleep," he says, grinning. "You know, pins and needles and that?"

Molly does not look impressed.

"Now," Jax continues, ignoring the ice glare, "we're *not* going to be spending the next two hours here, amirite? Can we have some agreement on this issue? Yes?"

Alice looks up, surprised. I'm not going to lie, the third eye takes a little getting used to.

"Where do you want to go?" she asks, her voice curious. She smiles, and I do a double take. While we were reading, she blacked out one of her teeth.

"NOWHERE!" Molly says loudly. "Nowhere, because we are NOT getting in more trouble. God! What's wrong with you?"

"Listen, you might be queen of the student council, but you have got to chill. Lewiston isn't coming back until lunch. And I'm not saying we're going far. I just figure . . . I got a stash in my locker that would make this whole thing more fun." Jax waggles his eyebrows, looking a little like that demonic goat god. What's his name? Pan. He looks like Pan, if Pan wore a flat brim.

"*DRUGS?*" Molly's voice drops, and even Erik and Andre stop what they're doing and stare.

Jax lowers his eyebrows and shakes his head in dis-appointment. "GIRL. You watch way too much TV. Skittles. And those caramel bull's-eye things. And chocolate-covered cranberries I stole from my dad's van, but he's supposed to be on a health kick anyway, so I'm doing him a favor."

"What's in the middle of those caramels?" Alice asks before anyone can respond. "I mean, it's white, it's sweet, but what *is* it? Does anyone know?"

We're all silent, pondering the mysteries of life and the sugary deliciousness of those bull's-eye candies.

"They're white magical angel tears, that's what," Jax announces with authority, and it's a sign of how far down the rabbit hole we've gone that all five of us nod along thoughtfully.

Molly, who I'm beginning to realize might have a bit of a thing for sugar, now has the look of someone impaled upon the horns of a massive moral dilemma.

"Where's your locker?" she asks finally. Her voice is the voice of regret and bad decisions.

I get it. On one hand, Jax is packing some seriously good stuff, and once again my lunch veered toward pathetic. On the other . . . I'm risking a breach in my most basic school rule: Don't get into anyone else's business. Stay out of it all—the dramas, the problems, the inside jokes, and the shenanigans.

This, no matter how I rationalize it, is shenanigans.

"By the gym. We won't even go near the front offices, and that's where Lewiston and Davis are," Jax says. He's finally stopped stomping and waits by the door. "Theo? Alice-girl? Who's in?"

I glance at Andre and he gives a tiny shrug.

"Fine," Molly snaps, getting up. "But we're going right to your locker and right back. Deal?"

Without discussion, Andre, Erik, Alice, and I stand up. Apparently, Molly speaks for all of us, at least on the matter of compromised morals and high-fructose corn syrup. To my relief, Erik walks toward the door with no more threatening attempts at eye contact.

Jax whoops. "Follow me, yo!" he says, opening the door. "And yo!" he stage-whispers back at us. "Stealth!"

Alice nods, her eyes wide.

Before I can reconsider, Jax gives another completely and 100 percent stealth-free whoop and runs down the hall.

We are not stealthy. At ALL.

If one were to create a chart representing stealth, with Wonder Woman's invisible jet at one end and the Pride parade in New York City at the other, we would be somewhere off the poster, near an 8.8-or-higher-on-the-Richter-scale earthquake.

No one seems to be around.

Jax goes tearing down the hall, occasionally leaping off the wall in a way that reminds me way too much of Otis the cat when he's lost his mind for no reason and goes careening around the house. The rest of us scuttle behind him, sticking close to the wall like, hilariously, that would make ANY difference when Jax is leading us like a one-man oompah band.

"WOULD YOU SHUT UP OH MY GOD WILL YOU PLEASE SHUT UP YOU GUYS PLEASE BE QUIET OH MY GOD," Molly whisper-shouts in a kind of constant stream-of-consciousness way.

We round the corner after Jax and immediately smash into him, one after another, like dominoes, or like a bad Three Stooges movie. Alice, who is last, falls backward and hits the floor with a squeak.

"Mr. Saunders. And some little kid. Back it up, and I mean right now," Jax whispers, and we pretty much crawl all over each other trying to get back down the hallway the way we came. Erik has to bodily lift Alice off the floor, because she appears to have lost a shoe *and* managed to spill her messenger bag. Again.

We skitter into the closest empty classroom, where Alice puts her shoe back on and the rest of us stare at each other. The mood is best described as treasonous panic.

"This. Is. A. TERRIBLE. Idea," Molly whispers.

We all stay silent. Mr. Saunders the janitor is the sort of kindly, smiling, friendly dude who teachers and students all like, and who gets the yearbook dedicated to him every few years. But beloved though he may be, none of us has any doubt of what will happen if he catches us.

His footsteps come closer. Alice squeaks again, barely audibly. Molly shoots her the patented I Am Freezing You with Ice Shards to Your Brain look, but Erik gives her arm a pat that I suppose is intended to be reassuring, though it looks like it might leave a bruise. Comforting? Threatening? Hard to know with Estrale.

"Nice to have your company, today, Li'l Bit. We'll finish up and go get some lunch, sound good?" He starts singing a peanut-butter-and-jelly song, and a boy—I guess his kid?— giggles. He's got a decent voice, actually, deep and smooth and kind of slow-jazz-style.

But the problem is, it's getting closer.

Before he gets to our door, the song breaks off. Instead, there's the sound of a fuzzy, static-filled walkie-talkie. The footsteps stop.

"Allo? What's up?" Mr. Saunders says, presumably into his walkie-talkie.

We all look at each other, except Andre, who's over by the teacher's desk. He mutters something that sounds like *"supply closet,"* but his hand is over his mouth and it's impossible to understand him.

"Anybody on here? You need me?" Mr. Saunders says outside the door. Then: "Shoot. Stupid technology. More trouble than it's worth. Teddy, we gotta walk down to maintenance anyway, since I can't understand the thing. I'm telling you, technology just makes more work. . . ."

His voice fades away as he walks, apparently toward the maintenance closet, which is by the cafeteria.

We all turn to stare at Andre.

"Kind of a dirty trick, but I wasn't sure what else to do," he says, and his face is sheepish.

"What DID you do?" Molly asks.

"Saved our butts, that's what he did! You. Are. A BEAST!" Jax says, leaping at Andre and giving him a hug that looks a little like a headlock.

Andre looks pained.

"I hit the 'maintenance' button on this thing a bunch of times and whispered 'supply closet.' Wasn't really sure what it would do," he admits.

I stare in admiration. But it's Erik who sums it up, or at least attempts to.

"Andre, man. There are team players and then there are *teammates,* and you, my friend, are the latter. I would throw you a no-look pass any day and twice on Sundays and trust you to get it and nail the shot, even if it were a three-pointer."

None of us knows quite how to respond to that, except Alice, who promptly says, "Same!"

Andre shrugs. But I think I see a smile threatening to break out.

Jax releases him and bounds toward the door. "Anyway, let's get back to the job at hand, right, people? Candy!"

"Skittles!" Molly adds.

"Caramel bull's-eyes," I say before I can stop myself.

Jax nods so vigorously his hat flies off. "Magical angel tears. Let's do this!"

And we're off again.

Back into the hallway, this time Jax going into Super-Stealth mode, bringing his knees up high and placing each foot down carefully, like the *Pink Panther* cartoon guy. One after another, we follow. Alice, I notice, lifts each knee exactly like Jax.

Finally we're at Jax's locker, which is right outside the gym. He opens it and pulls out a crumpled bag full of candy.

"Did you *steal* that?" Molly asks, her face a war between avarice and You Deeply Disappoint Me.

"Naw, that's you, remember?" Jax says, smiling so big that it takes a minute for Molly to get it.

"Shut up! That was once, and I had to—"

"Kidding! Just a joke. I'm messing with you," Jax says, and his smile is real.

Molly is back to Def Con Scarlet, but she gives a kind of half smile back. "I know you were kidding," she mumbles.

Meanwhile, we are too close to the gym for Erik to handle, and he's making fidgety freak-out motions that look like a mix between a toddler who reallyreallyreally has to go to the bathroom and a cat trying to barf. (Also, I will note here that the motion of a cat gakking up a hairball, when set to dubstep, is oddly compelling.)

"Duuuuuuudes. I'm just . . . We gotta go in. For a little bit!"

"Absolutely not," Molly snaps. "We should get back before—"

"What's *in* there?" Alice interrupts, standing on tiptoe to look through the small window. "I don't think I've ever been in."

We all turn and stare at her, even Molly, who's got one hand in the bag of Skittles.

"I don't really do sporty things," Alice says, blinking (two of her three eyes), her voice as cheerful as ever.

"We *have* to do sporty things," Andre says. "I don't do them either, but it's not a choice."

I nod. In this matter, at least, we are Nerds United. I skateboard and got up to a brown belt in karate and can swim a mile at the pool, so I'm not a slug. But team sports, or even the sadly clichéd horror of PE dodgeball and floor hockey . . . not so much.

Alice shrugs. "I just . . . don't really do it."

I think about this. Alice is wack enough that she might have some special weirdo way of getting out of PE that works only if you regularly come to school in a tutu or wear six pigtails in your hair.

Erik has been watching us with the kind of expression usually reserved for watching the Jaws of Life pull a motionless body out of a totaled car.

"But ... sports are LIFE. They're EVERYTHING! They're where the good guys get to beat the bad guys, and where you stand up for your teammates even if you don't even like the dude outside of the game. And where everyone does his best for the team, even if it means sacrificing yourself. THERE'S NO *I* IN *TEAM*! I mean, that says it all!"

Andre and I exchange startled looks. Erik's a little dangerous, spit flying out of his mouth as he spews his clichés. I'm tempted to explain to him that it's not exactly nirvana for those of us who are more likely to *be* the target than shoot for the target, but I don't want to get into it with him when he's this frenzied. I settle for rolling my eyes, which, if it were a sport, I would be on the Olympic podium.

"That's it," Erik says, looking from face to face. "We're goin' in."

Given the new trend of threatening eye contact, I'm not about to be the one to defy him.

"Little fuel for the game ahead?" Jax says brightly, offering around the bag.

I grab a handful of caramels and start unwrapping them. Shoving one in my mouth, I look at Andre and Molly again and shrug.

Molly, who's scowling so hard it looks like she tried to bunch all her features into the center of her face, shrugs back.

Erik opens the door to the gym, and the smell of several civilizations' worth of sweaty gym socks hits us like a slap of olfactory nightmare.

Everyone cringes, except Erik, who takes a deep breath. "This!" he cries, gesturing us in. "This is the smell of joy!"

We are all too busy breathing through our mouths to answer.

CHAPTER 15

Let's Hope the Olympic Committee Hasn't Finalized the 2020 Summer Games

It turns out you can get used to the smell of fermenting gym socks pretty quickly. Or maybe the delightful miasma of Skittles and chocolate overwhelms it. The fact is, once we realize that we're the only ones in the gym, and no postpubescent, recently-started-shaving thirteen-year-old fascist is going to give us wedgies or dome us with the medicine balls, it's actually not awful.

That's not quite true. It's more than not-awful. It's pretty freaking epic.

First Erik—again acting oddly human and decent—takes Alice to the middle of the basketball court and shows her how to shoot a free throw. She squeaks and refuses to catch it when he throws the basketball to her, which slows the process down a bit. But finally he carefully places it on the floor a few feet away and rolls it to her. It stops right at her feet, and after staring at it for a few seconds like it's a Magic 8 Ball, she picks it up and starts shooting. At the other end, Molly's gotten out a soccer ball and is crashing it toward the back wall like she's got a personal grudge against black-and-white spheres. She's pretty excellent at it, not surprisingly, since her Overachiever status extends to sports. And she really seems to get a lot of happiness out of nailing that thing again and again.

I stay far away.

The rest of us get the giant yoga balls out of the pen where they're kept and roll back and forth on our stomachs. But then Erik gets the idea of yoga-ball soccer.

"Three to a team! Me, Alice, and Andre versus Theo, Jax, and Molly!" He takes a running leap toward his yoga ball and overshoots, flying off the front of it and landing with a huge, hollow crash.

We all freeze.

"*OH MAN,*" Jax whisper-shouts. "If there's blood, we are so screwed."

But Erik pops up again with a spectacular red bump on his head. "My bad! But no worries. Let's do this!"

"Let's put a little skin in the game," Jax says, rolling quite gracefully over to the candy bag. "Let's say . . . play to twenty, and winning team gets the candy bag."

"Ten," Molly says quickly, rolling expertly behind him. "We have GOT to get back or we're dead."

I try to mount my yoga ball and meet them center court but manage to get my foot stuck under it and make a loud foot-fart noise, then fall sideways off the ball.

Jax nods thoughtfully like this is a technique I might want to teach the rest of them. "Theo, you're going to be, like, goalie. You stay put."

Never have I been so gracefully told I suck.

Not surprisingly, Alice is the other team's "goalie," i.e., designated pathetic non–yoga ball rock star. What is surprising is that Andre is not that bad. He scuttles around on his ball like some kind of beetle, his long arms and legs reaching around easily. He scores on me once, and I stop a second goal—an impressive combination of my flailing in the right direction while simultaneously giving the kind of war cry Satan's minion might make if he hadn't hit puberty yet that I think throws him off his shot. Then Jax gets serious, guarding him closely, chirping at him the whole time. Jax, I have to add, is the king of the chirp. Some choice samples:

"Son, I'm going to be the milk in your cereal, the change in your pocket, the gum in your mouth. You even think of shooting and I'll be there."

"Andre, we might as well be related, you know? Because I'll be all up in your business right through Christmas. You hear Santa? That'll be me, hanging out by the chimney with your stocking."

"You know your blood type, Andre? Because close as we are now, you might want to make sure we're *compatible*!"

After this last one, Andre falls off his ball from laughing too hard, and Jax quickly scores two goals before the other team can pull it together.

At one point the other team seems to be everywhere at once, and they score three goals in a row, and when I scream for a time-out, I look over and Molly and Jax are sitting on the bleachers with the bag of candy between them. Molly doesn't even look guilty.

"Go team!" she yells.

After a quick time-out, where I dig deep for the best pep talk possible ("If you could *not* hang me out to dry like somebody's stained underwear, that'd be *great*"), we're back at it.

Molly faces off against Alice this time, which should be embarrassingly easy, except that Molly gives a most pathetic squeal, and Alice is past her like the world's least graceful crab. I brace for her shot, but when she gets to me, I too give a pathetic squeal, and she scores immediately.

That's when we make the rule that it's illegal to put a fake severed finger in a nostril.

The game ends with Erik pushing past Jax, committing an egregious foul that would get him disqualified from official soccer-yoga competition for a decade if anyone had seen it, and scoring a winning goal. I brace for the anger and disappointment of my teammates, only to find that during their break they've eaten a cool half of the candy already so aren't too fussed about the result.

The sugar has so chilled Molly out that she barely even freaks on the way back to the classroom.

As we tiptoe through the hallway, Erik gives me one of those dude-punches on the arm.

"Admit it, that was sick," he says.

I shrug-nod, not willing to admit that I haven't laughed that hard in years, but also not willing to flat out lie to the guy who gave me my first dude-punch. (It stings a little more than I expected.)

"Come *on*! Teamwork! Fun!"

"Candy!" Molly interjects.

"I thought it was totally fun," Alice says. Thankfully, she's taken the fake finger out of her nose. Bad news is that she's tucked it behind her ear for safekeeping, and the jagged severed edge is sticking out. I avert my eyes.

"It was," I admit. "It was pretty excellent."

Erik punches me again, and I try not to flinch. "Told you," he crows. "You should join a team. It's just . . . it's the best."

I think about telling him that yoga-ball soccer is not yet a recognized sport, but somehow I can't summon my usual snark. Total truth? He's like a Labrador retriever . . . so excited you can practically see his tail wagging (metaphorically speaking, of course). It's hard not to fall for it.

"Sports are a pretty big deal to you, I guess," I say. This is up there with the most obvious statements ever made, second only to the famous "Wow! That's water!" statement by Dave Howe during the second-grade burst-pipe debacle.

But Erik nods vigorously, like I've said something enlightening and intelligent. "Most important thing in my life," he says, and for once his voice doesn't sound like a Gatorade ad. He sounds . . . serious, and a little sad.

I'm so startled that I blurt out my next question without thinking. "Why? I mean, why's it such a big deal?"

Erik slows a little, so that Jax, Molly, and Andre are a little ahead. Alice is still behind us. When I turn around, she's lifting up her knees and taking exaggerated tiptoe steps again.

"You wouldn't get it," Erik says.

"Because I'm not a jock, you mean." I roll my eyes. "Right. Secret handshakes and all that. Sorry." I speed up, ready to get away.

Erik speeds up right next to me, though. "No! That's not what I meant. Because you're not . . . because you're smart." He sighs. "Look. I'm really good at sports. Like, I've got natural talent, *and* I work. Wicked hard. And"—he pauses, glances at Alice, who's still right behind us, apparently high-knee-tiptoeing faster to keep up—"well, let's just say I'm *not* that good at school. Like, I'm dyslexic. Do you even know what that means?"

I nod, though I'm not totally sure.

"It doesn't mean I'm stupid," he says quickly.

"I know," I say just as fast. "Words look weird to you, right?"

"Words *and* numbers. Yeah. It's hard to read and write normally, so everything takes way longer, and it's . . . Like I said, I'm not that good at it."

I slow back down and glance at him. "But . . . you're supposed to get help for that. Doesn't the school—"

He interrupts, waving a hand impatiently. "Yeah, yeah, yeah. I have all that stuff. I have a tutor and all these accommodations. Like when Lewiston brought me that tape player. I can listen to the readings and stuff." He pauses. "But still. Everyone in my family is wicked smart. Like Harvard smart. And that's not going to be me, even with the tutors and everything." He's quiet again. "I'm nothing like them."

By now we're at the classroom, and the others are inside. Molly's waving at us.

"Come *on*!" she says, her The World Is Too Idiotic for

Me to Handle voice coming back. "Ms. Lewiston isn't here yet, but she'll probably be back any minute. *Move!*" She ducks back into the room.

Erik and I pause outside the door, Alice right behind us.

We all kind of stare at the floor, then at each other. My eyes accidentally snag on the severed finger again, and I snort-laugh, shaking my head a little.

Erik sees the finger too and laughs.

Alice laughs too. Then she takes the finger and shoves it back up her nose.

"I'm not really like my family either," she says.

When Ms. Lewiston comes in, apologizing for how long it all took and telling us it's time for lunch, we're all sitting silently reading (or in Erik's case, listening) and making notes. If she notices the faint smell of candy and sweat, she must attribute it to the permanent funk of the room.

"We'll circle up now," she says. "And I want to say I really appreciate the dedication you're showing to the process. I know it was a lot to ask you to be alone in here, and I'm grateful that you honored my trust."

I stare at her through my hair, trying to see if this is some kind of reverse-psychology move. But she looks earnest. I very definitely and clearly don't look at my dishonorable classmates. I hear Alice give a faint squeak, and I close my eyes briefly, hoping that will be the end of it.

But Molly's not one to leave a potentially reputation-ruining silence alone. "It was useful," she says. "You know, having the time without you. I mean! Not *without* you, but without any talking. Quiet. Silence. Noiselessness." She gulps. "NO NOISE!"

Code Red! Molly apparently has ZERO game when it comes to playing it cool with teachers. She is the worst delinquent in the history of delinquents.

I flash a panicked look at Jax, who rolls his eyes.

"Jeepus, what a rookie," he mutters under his breath. "It's all good, Ms. Lewiston," he says, louder. "We got the story read, and even got Theo here to talk. You know, tell us all about his photos and stuff. Feels like, I don't know, we bonded."

Ms. Lewiston's eyebrow, which began its Everest-height climb during Molly's endless rambling, goes even higher.

But Jax is a pro. He grins and pulls his chair toward the center of the room. "It's good, right? I mean, it's all part of the process."

Erik follows his lead and slings his bag over his shoulder. "Yeah, I think we're getting somewhere."

Alice squeaks again.

Ms. Lewiston looks at me. I pull my fedora on and look down at my backpack, taking longer than needed to put my pencil and story away.

Finally she nods and sits down. "Great. That's great to hear," she says, and her voice is hard to read, but we don't care, because we're all too busy avoiding each other's eyes to pay attention.

CHAPTER 16

People Start to Freak Out, but Don't Worry, I'll Just Start Maniacally Talking About Pinhole Cameras

When we're finally all in place, Ms. Lewiston has her bag of Starburst back out.

"How's everyone doing?" she asks, and it's notable that instead of doing the mumble-shrug nonanswer, all six of us actually respond, calling out variations on "Good," "Cool," "Okay," and "HEY, MORE STARBURST!" (Three guesses on who that last one is, first two guesses that aren't Molly don't count.)

"Good!" Ms. Lewiston smiles. "And yes, my stash is back out. Anyway," she says, and maybe I'm imagining the slightly knowing look in her eye, "I brought treats because it's time to really unpack what's going on here."

Jax catches my eye and mouths, quite clearly, *"Rematch . . . bring it on."*

I burst out laughing and turn it into a fake cough.

"Sorry," I say-cough. "Coffee went down the wrong tube." I keep hacking for another few seconds to legitimize my claim, but when I look up, Ms. Lewiston has moved on.

"It's time for honesty," Ms. Lewiston says, and now no one is laughing. "It's time to admit mistakes, acknowledge wrongs, and realize that we all need to move forward."

I look back down at my desk, all laughter gone. Stupid. Rookie-level stupid. I had allowed that school version of Stockholm syndrome to cloud my judgment so that I actually felt chill, like these are my people. They aren't. Or at least, one of them isn't. And if it isn't Erik, if he's actually not like his dipwad friends, well . . . that means someone *else* hates me. And somehow that doesn't make me feel any better. My stomach clenches, and I straighten up and let my hair fall over my face.

Ms. Lewiston's voice is soft. "The goal of the past few days has been to get you six to see each other with new eyes, to question your own assumptions about each other, and to learn to trust one another." She looks around. "I hope we've succeeded somewhat on that front."

People mutter and nod, but I stay silent. The fact is, I *did* learn more about my classmates than I have in seven years of togetherness. And I *did* trust them, sort of. But now we're back here, where Erik, or one of the others, has to admit they hate my photos enough to ruin them. Twice.

Ms. Lewiston goes on. "Some things to think about before we proceed. One is that intentions are often different from results. We learned that when we talked about lying, and what happens next. Another is that we often don't know everything about why someone took the actions he or she did. When we discussed the story, we saw how that can play out. It's possible he—or she—didn't mean to cause harm."

Molly looks up. Her cheeks are flaming red again.

"He or she? Do you really think me or Alice did this? I mean, does this seem like something *I* would do?" She looks around. "And if we're being *honest,* I think we all know that." She looks at Jax and Erik for a second, then looks away.

Jax leans back. "What's that supposed to mean? You're too perfect to mess up? You'd probably rather die than ever get in trouble, is that right?"

I wince a little at the word *die.* Though obviously we all say things like "I almost died," now that I know about Molly's brother, I can't help wondering if that word feels like a slap every time.

"Shut up," Molly hisses. "You don't know anything."

"You sure? I'm betting I can be pretty clear on what's going on at the Claremont household." Jax stands up and, in a high voice, imitates Molly's mother.

"Hi, honey! I'm home! Is our little Molly-kins here?"

Then he's her father: "Hi, darling! How was your day at the office? And of course Molly-kins is here! Where else would she be?"

"Of course she's here! She's perfect!"

"Perfect!"

"SHUT UP!" Molly screams, also standing up.

Ms. Lewiston jumps to her feet. "Jax! Molly!" She puts a hand on Molly's shoulder. Molly has tears streaming down her cheeks.

Jax stares at the ground, breathing hard.

"Both of you, take a walk with me. Now." With that they leave the room, the no-slam door shutting silently behind them.

Erik, Andre, Alice, and I stare at each other.

Alice speaks first. "That wasn't very nice of Jax," she says, but instead of sounding angry or gossipy, she sounds curious. "I wonder why he did it?"

Erik shrugs, a quick, angry gesture. "Who knows? I mean, it did sort of feel like Molly was accusing him or me, but . . ." He trails off. "You win or lose before the game starts, you know?"

There's a meditative silence while we ponder this.

Alice blinks (two of the three eyes) and says what I suspect Andre and I are both thinking: "No, I don't really know."

Erik looks surprised that we're not fluent in jock. "Oh. Well . . . I mean, it's all in the mindset, right? If you're in a bad headspace, it's really hard to focus and bring any winning energy to the game. You got to have your head there first."

To my surprise, Andre nods at this. "Same as playing live or even recording. If you don't get your head into the music, it doesn't work. You have to be totally *there,* you know? You have to commit."

I look at Alice and shrug. I don't think photography is like that. I don't have to get my "head in the game" or "commit" or whatever.

While we wait, I go through my backpack, mostly so I don't have to stare at the three people left in the room. I pull out my latest pinhole camera and start fussing with it. It's a pretty simple one, a big old tin that used to hold crackers or something that I found at a yard sale. It's big enough that I'm hoping to try again with what went so wrong in the darkroom—a really long-exposure photo.

Alice leans over. "What is that?"

"Just a pinhole camera. You know, like we did in photography last semester."

Andre squints at it. "Except ours didn't look anything like that."

Erik looks too. "Seriously. Ours were little plastic nothings. That's, like . . . cool."

Alice nods, and her third eye wobbles. "That looks so rad! It's like something out of a steampunk movie," she says. "What are you going to take a photo of?"

I shrug. I actually had an idea to take the words Ms. Lewiston had written on the board, about everyone fighting a battle we can't see, and frame them in low light and shoot that. But I didn't want to say that for some reason.

"Oh! You could do a sick shot of a tree," Erik says, his voice cracking in excitement. "Think about it. You could, like, shoot from below into the branches!"

I look at him, trying to get a read on whether this is sarcasm. If it were me, I can guarantee it would be sarcasm. But he looks like an eager puppy who's waiting for a tennis ball. It's increasingly hard to believe he's playing me.

Mentally I shrug. Even though his idea is totally clichéd (plus, where are we supposed to find a tree in here?), I feel I should compliment him on taking baby steps toward something not sportsball-related.

"That would be cool," I say, admirably keeping my snark on a tight leash. "But I was thinking about shooting something in this room. Maybe lighting something with really low light and leaving it for a superlong exposure."

Erik nods slowly, like I said something insightful about point guards or defense. And I realize we're both being kind.

"Here," I say, scooting closer. "Do you remember in class when Mr. Smith told us how these things work? It's a pretty basic setup. The smaller the pinhole, the less light, so the longer the exposure to light you need. But there's one more variable, right?" I don't wait for an answer. "Because the size of the camera matters. . . . If it's a big box like this one, and a tiny hole, and I use really low light—like, almost-darkness low light . . . well, I could set it to 'take' the picture over ten or even fifteen hours."

Andre and Alice move their chairs closer.

When Ms. Lewiston opens the door, we're all huddled over my desk, where I'm showing them how to load the photo paper.

Jax saunters over. "Yo, what's going on here? You building a robot?" His voice is casual and jokey, but there's a new quietness in how he moves.

Molly comes in silently behind him and looks over my shoulder.

"I'm almost done. I was making a pinhole camera and talking about how I want to set up a long-exposure shot. Like, seriously long, as in, overnight long. And see if I can use really low light but still get a cool result."

Jax and Molly nod like they know what I'm talking about and it matters to them.

"Actually," I continue, because apparently when I'm nervous and people seem to be actually listening to me I get verbal diarrhea, "I have some other materials in my bag, so maybe I'll make a few cameras"—I look around—"or, you know, you guys could help—"

Alice nods so hard the severed finger flies out from behind her ear. "That would be so cool! And if you made a bunch of them, you could set up a few different shots with that long-exposure thing you were talking about and see which ones come out best."

I glance at Ms. Lewiston, who's watching us.

"Would that be okay?" I ask. I want to say, "Can we please do something slightly more enjoyable than this circle thing, like perhaps stabbing ourselves repeatedly in the eyes with forks?" But I don't.

Ms. Lewiston nods. "I have to make a quick phone call, so I'm going to step out into the hall. Why don't you work on the cameras until I get back." She looks around. "And at the end of the day we'll get back into circle and see if anyone is ready to share. So think on that while you're working."

I look up at the clock. It's less than an hour until dismissal. I can't help wondering: Will today end with a confession? Will we be done with this—four people declared innocent, and someone here, someone who's been pretend-ing to open up and admitting that they did it? And then what? I'm still here, my stuff still ruined, but with a name to go with this idea of a bully? A name and a face and their favorite candy and all sorts of other facts I didn't know until this week? Will that help? Really?

As my fingers move over the pieces of the cameras, I let my mind go to photography, to the science of light and dark and framing and perspective. As I talk and work, I realize that part of me doesn't want to know the truth today. If we set up these cameras, I'll need to come back tomorrow any-way. Seems weird to think that no one else would be here to see them.

CHAPTER 17

I Nerd Out on Photography, but Everyone's Cool with That, or at Least Pretends to Be

When Ms. Lewiston leaves, we all relax a little. Molly and Jax don't talk to each other much, but they're both more mellow, like Ms. Lewiston did some Jedi mind trick on them and chilled them both out.

Jax looks at the tin box camera. "That's pretty dope," he says. "What are you planning for that one?"

I shrug. "Not sure yet. I want to leave them overnight, but I have to figure out how to keep the light levels constant, and low enough that it isn't a white blob."

Alice squeaks. "Oh! What about the fake-candle thing that Ms. Lewiston uses for our circles? You could do something awesome with that, right? I mean, maybe you can use it to light the edge of a knife, and have a drop of blood on it, which could reflect the light. Though if it's really slow exposure, maybe the blood would dry and be flat. So in that case, we might want to use nail polish. . . ." She trails off as she notices that we're all staring at her. "What?" she asks, scowling.

I don't quite know where to start, but Molly says gently, "You know we can't have knives in school, right?"

Erik nods so vigorously I think he might injure himself. "That's true. Aidan on the soccer team . . . he had a Swiss Army knife in his backpack from a camping trip and he was sent home for the day even though it was his dad's! But"— Erik gets a little pink and mumbly—"I still think that was a really cool idea. I mean, if we could, I think it would be awesome."

Alice beams. "*Thank* you!"

Interesting.

Still, I have work to do if I'm going to get these things set up before we have to go home or, worse, circle up again for another round of "Who hates poor Theo?"

I poke around in my bag. "It looks like I have enough stuff for four cameras, though each one will be a little different. Here's the thing: when you want to do a long exposure like this, not only do you have to make it a pretty big camera, relatively speaking, and make the hole pretty small, but you also need some kind of filter."

"Isn't overnight going to be way too long?" Andre asks.

"I mean, when we did pinhole cameras in art, I think the longest we ever left them was five minutes, maybe?"

I nod. "Yeah, we did—"

Jax interrupts. "And that was the one where I totally whiffed it and forgot to make the second hole, so basically got nothing. I tried to tell Smitty that it was a picture of the Black Experience, but he wasn't buying." He shakes his head and gives a barking not-funny laugh. "Just another total fail."

I look at Jax. "If it makes you feel any better, when I first got to use a serious film camera, like the kind professionals use, I went out for three hours in the neighborhood, setting up shots, getting all serious about framing them and stuff, and moving around shooting from different angles like some kind of rock-star photographer. All I needed was the scarf and the man-purse to be, like, an Italian superstar."

Jax snorts, and I laugh too, shaking my head.

"When I got home, all psyched and fired up to get into the darkroom, I realized I had never loaded the film properly in the first place. I literally hadn't taken a single shot the whole three hours I was out there jumping around like Ansel Adams on Red Bull."

The others laugh, and Erik shakes his head, saying,

"Classic mistake. Gotta prep the field before you can play ball," which I ignore.

But Jax looks at me, his face scrunched. "That must have straight up bummed you out," he says. "I mean, did you ever get to take those photographs?"

I shake my head. "Naw. But honestly, they weren't that great. They were, like, arty tree shots and stuff." Oops. I quickly glance at Erik, but he's too busy visualizing prepping the field (what?!) or whatever to notice I'm dissing his tree-branch idea.

"Anyway," I say, "point is that in photography, there are always screwups. And yeah, it can be a huge downer when you think you've missed some once-in-a-lifetime shot, but—"

Erik interrupts. " 'You miss one hundred percent of the shots you don't take!' " He sounds WAY too excited.

I look at him. "Um . . . yeah, that's a good way of putting it, I guess."

"Wayne Gretzky. The Great One. That's what he said, and man, it's like, my . . . my . . ."

"Your mantra," Alice says.

"Your guiding principle," Molly says.

"Your bumper sticker," I mutter, and Andre and Jax both snort-laugh.

Erik turns pink, and I feel a little bad. Looking at him biting his lip and staring at his desk, I wonder again if I could have gotten it totally wrong.

"No, seriously, it's a good motto," I say. "It's true. If you worry too much about setting up the shot, or messing with the lighting, or even whether your equipment is any good, you'll never actually press the button and take the picture." I stand up and start pacing. "And that's the thing—nowadays most people shoot digital, and they can take literally thousands and thousands of photos without even switching out a memory card or battery. Which is great, and means everyone can take a million pictures and hopefully get something good."

Erik starts to speak, probably to say something about swinging at the ball or shooting the puck, but I'm on a roll and I ride right over him.

"But that takes some of the magic—and the risk—out of it. When I shoot film, and especially when I use pinhole cameras, I only get a limited number of shots. With the pinhole I might only get one try, ever. So I have to balance that risk . . . not taking the shot versus wasting my shot. You know? That's what makes it fun."

They're all staring at me, and all of a sudden I have the same feeling I had when we were supposed to sing "This

Land Is Your Land" in music and I belted it out, all the way through the second verse, before I realized we were singing only the chorus. I immediately let my hair fall in front of my face.

But Alice is nodding thoughtfully. "I know *exactly* what you mean," she says. "When I'm filming, especially if it's an outdoor shot with heavy special effects, I have to figure out how to get the best possible performance from the actors before their blood dries or the bruises start to gray out. You know? The worst thing is when we spend forever getting it right, and getting the mats into place so whoever is being stabbed or thrown from a building can fall safely, and then, right when we're set and everyone's totally ready, some idiot dog walker comes through!"

She looks about as angry as I've ever seen her. With the extra eye, it's particularly creepy, and suddenly I get how she might star as the killer in her slasher films.

"It's *always* the dog walkers," she hisses.

Silence while the rest of us carefully don't make eye contact, in case she's about to go serial killer on us. My alarm grows.

Then she grins again and does her HEE-HEE laugh. "Was that creepy? That was a line from my last movie, where I *totally* got revenge. I think I killed off, like, four dog walkers in that one. And a bunch of dogs."

Again silence reigns as we all process Alice's murder of Shipton's numerous parka-and-snow-boot-wearing dog walkers.

She waves a hand impatiently. "Actors, obviously. Anyway, moving on."

I blink and catch Andre's eye, and his expression mimics what I'm feeling. I would characterize it as an I Don't Even Know What the Right Expression Should Be for This Scenario but I'm Getting Nervous face.

I jump in.

"Thanks, Alice," I say, which doesn't make sense but seems better than trying to unpack her dog-walking hatred. "I, uh . . . yeah. Totally."

Everyone is looking a little lost. Jax has wandered over to his backpack and is methodically pulling out what appears to be a massive pile of Matchbox cars. Everyone else is still hanging out by my camera but standing around like they can't remember why they're here.

"Anyway. The cameras," I say, and I don't think it's my imagination that Molly and Erik look relieved. "I was just messing around with this one, but if you guys want . . . I mean, I can make a few others. Just, you know, to kill time."

To my surprise, it's Jax who speaks up first, and loudly. "Yeah, let's do it. I bet you can make something totally lit. I'm down to help, so, you know . . . what do you need?"

I look over at him. He's surrounded by the Matchbox cars, a bunch of Starburst wrappers, and a stack of notebooks.

"Well," I say slowly, "I'm not sure why you have a bunch of toy cars, and I'm not judging you—"

"Dude, they're my *brother's.* He's always hiding stuff in my bag when he's supposed to clean up," Jax says, rolling his eyes.

I can't help it. I grin. "Sure they are. Well, your 'brother's cars'"—I make air quotes with my fingers—"could make a good subject, if we set them up right."

Jax fake scowls. "If they were my cars, I would *own* that! I would declare, loud and proud, that I brought my best Matchbox cars in. And I wouldn't bring this sad . . . What is this?" he examines one of the cars. "This *Pinto* or whatever the heck. I'd be rolling in with my Lambo or Bugatti." He shakes his head, pretending to be annoyed. "Yo, if I bring my Matchbox cars, you'll know."

I nod seriously. "Yeah. Good to know you keep your best ones at home. Probably in a glass curio cabinet with special lighting."

He bursts out laughing.

"And you maybe even go down to Boston to the Convention Center, for when they have those classic toy sales. I hear those places are totally hype. Great place to meet the ladies too, if you know what I mean."

It should be noted that when Jax chooses a car to throw at my head, he does, in fact, throw a Ford Pinto. Luckily, he misses.

"Enough!" Molly shouts, with only a fraction of her usual You Are All Too Stupid to Be Alive voice. "Are you going to show us how to make these cameras or what?"

I look at her. She's standing with Alice, Erik, and Andre.

"Uh, sure," I say, silently tossing the Pinto back into Jax's backpack. "Let's get started."

CHAPTER 18

It's Possible We'll Create Moving Works of Art but Also Possible They Will Be Epically Awful. As Usual.

Ms. Lewiston comes in five minutes before dismissal, clearly frazzled.

"Apologies, apologies," she says, rushing over. "Ms. Davis . . ." She pauses and takes a deep breath. "Ms. Davis needed my assistance with something, and I'm afraid we're out of time."

We're all crouched around the fourth and last (and most complicated) pinhole camera, a totally wack foldable one that we decided to set up facing the Matchbox car, filtered to try to get a funky vintage effect.

It's almost done and would probably be finished already, except Alice somehow managed to create a massive fake slash across her cheek while the rest of us were looking at the camera, and when Molly saw it, she startled so badly she knocked off the front piece, which had taken ten minutes to attach.

Honestly, it was worth it. Alice is pretty awesome.

Anyway, Ms. Lewiston looks at us and then at the clock, then sighs. "I really *am* sorry for this. But we aren't going to have time to circle back up. So unless someone wants to share before we pack up, I'm afraid we're going to have to come back tomorrow."

She looks around. "I was really hoping we were getting somewhere, and we might be able to wrap up today so you could have the second half of your vacation week."

We're all quiet. I have nothing to say and don't really want to look around at the five faces to see if I can guess whether someone looks guilty. Despite my best attempts, though, my eyes fly up. I meet Andre's, and he gives a half grin.

"It's cool," he says. "I kind of want to see how these photos come out anyway."

Molly, Erik, and Jax all nod.

"Same, bro," Jax says. "I'm not saying anything, but I *think* that Matchbox shot has *Pulitzer* written all over it."

Alice raises her hand. "Oh! I think the skull one is going to be the best! I mean, come on!"

The skull one *will* be sick, if it works. Though I admit,

when Alice brightly announced she had a mouse skull in her bag if we wanted it for a photo, I was at a loss. There's really no good answer to "Do you want to use my mouse skull?" other than "Sure." But it may actually be awesome.

So the four shots are:

1) Mouse skull on the windowsill
2) Matchbox car posed on a diorama of the Grand Canyon we found on a bookshelf
3) Ms. Lewiston's quote, rewritten in fancy script on a piece of construction paper that Molly did some complicated scissors work to so that it looks kind of like a snowflake, and taped to the wall down low by the floor
4) Closet door with a fake candle inside it

Ms. Lewiston smiles, and her frazzle-dom seems to ease a little. "Well, thank you for being gracious. And, Theo, those cameras look fascinating. I can't wait to see how the images come out. Will you be able to show us tomorrow?"

I nod. "Yeah, as long as we can go to the darkroom for a little bit in the morning." I turn to the others. "But remember—no guarantees they won't be a total fail. I mean, that's the risk with these things. So I don't know—"

Jax cuts me off. "It's all good. Dude, I can write a novel

about things that are supposed to be great turning to a pile of fecal matter." He shrugs. "It's cool to see what happens."

I nod, trying not to give my cheesy smile that makes me look like a five-year-old chipmunk. But I kind of want to. This is actually turning out to be fun.

I close the blinds so the room will be mostly dark, and Ms. Lewiston ushers us all out, turning out the lights behind her. I look back before the door closes and can faintly see the fake candle flickering in the closet. It's a dull gray winter day, and the light is warmer and brighter than you'd think a tiny little drugstore light would be.

As we walk out toward the driveway, Molly's lecturing Andre on the benefits of joining the school band while Andre politely nods. But when I catch his eye, he makes a never-in-a-million-years face at me, and I snort-laugh.

"What?" Molly says, scowling. "Are you laughing at school band? Because I'll have you know, we're actually pretty good. And there's a jazz band too. Plus we play for the school musicals . . ." She goes on, but I escape by walking faster and catching up with Alice. *Sorry, Andre, dude. But it's every man for himself when Molly's on a school-spirit rampage.*

Alice beams at me. "You know, this is turning into a really fun week," she says, her happy face only partly mangled by the fake slash and dried blood.

Erik overhears. "It *is* pretty good," he says, and once again his cheeks go blotchy pink.

Dude. I think Erik might be getting like-like feelings for Alice.

"I can't wait to see those photos," Alice continues, apparently oblivious to her enticing appeal to Erik, who appears to be tripping over the pattern on the tiles. Since he's literally the most coordinated human being I've ever seen, I have to assume he's having an Alice attack. Guy seriously needs to get some chill.

"You know what might be cool," I say to Alice, sending telepathy messages to Erik to pull himself together, "you could set up some really creepy pinhole-camera shots as kind of . . . I don't know . . . teasers for your movies."

Alice stops suddenly and turns to face me, causing Erik to slam into her. Of course she drops her messenger bag with a squeak, and she and Erik both get down on their knees to rescue her five million pencil cases and notebooks and, yes, what look like at least a dozen tampons.

"Sorry, sorry, sorry," Erik is muttering, trying to shove stuff back into the bag without acknowledging anyone or anything. He's now achieved Molly levels of redness.

"Oh, it's okay. I probably shouldn't stop so suddenly. People are always slamming into me. And at least you smell good." She takes a deep inhale, and Erik drops the pens he's holding with a clatter. "Like pine or something."

Erik's face is approaching nuclear fusion. "My dad buys balsam soap," he mumbles.

I cough a totally fake theatrical DUDE, I'M RIGHT HERE cough.

"Anyway, the photos . . . ," I hint, and Alice stands up smiling, apparently unaware that she has completely incapacitated Erik.

"Right! I love that idea. I'm thinking about entering one of my shorts in the Shipton Film Festival this year, so that would be perfect. Will you help me? It's going to be a kind of update of Poe's 'The Tell-Tale Heart.'"

I look at Erik, wondering if he knows the Edgar Allan Poe story of the dude who put a still-beating heart in the walls of a house. It's gothic and weird and creepy and awesome, not unlike Alice herself. "That sounds rad," I say. "Erik, your idea about the . . . bare tree branches before was really . . . um . . . funky. Maybe you want to work on this?"

Erik finally lumbers to his feet like Frankenstein's monster, and for a second I think he's going to just monster-walk away. But he gulps so loud I can hear it and finally says, "Cool."

That's all he manages, but I *think* what he means is

"Dude, you are an A-plus wingman, and I so appreciate you helping me out when I have all the game of a recently neutered orangutan." But maybe I'm projecting.

By the time we get out front we're full of ideas for creepy shots, and Alice doesn't seem to notice that whoever's in the gold Lexus is honking at her.

After the fifth extended *honnnnnnnnnk,* she looks up, startled.

"Oh! Is that—"

"Someone seems to be in a rush," I say politely, as though this is not the act of a seriously rude toddler.

Alice shrugs and shoulders her bag. Her fingers gently touch her fake slash. "Yeah. He usually is." She walks toward the car. "See you tomorrow!" she calls over her shoulder.

Like before, the car pulls away almost before she closes the door. Turning away from the driveway, I nearly run into Erik, who's standing weirdly close to me. I take a step back.

"Um . . . ," I start. The sweaty-armpit feeling is back, and I can't help thinking that it would seriously suck if he chose right now, outside the school and away from Ms. Lewiston, to go all Hulk-smash-psycho on me. But he just stares at me, breathing hard.

I start getting scared for real. I want to walk away, but I'm stuck, hypnotized-mouse-in-the-glare-of-an-owl-style.

He opens his mouth, and I brace myself. "Listen," he starts.

I flinch and wrap my arms around my stomach. His voice does *not* sound good. But before he can say more, a Toyota pulls up fast, tires scraping against the curb, and the window opens. "ERIK. If you want a ride to that stupid basketball thing you're so obsessed with, we need to go *now*!" a voice calls. "Mom said I had to get you, but I'm in the middle of a review session, so let's GO."

Erik blinks, and a weird look—anger? relief? sadness? I can't tell—comes over his face.

"Yo, see you tomorrow, bro," he says, giving me yet another dude-punch and loping off to the car.

I stare after him, too confused and relieved to answer. But Erik doesn't look back; he's staring at his phone as the car pulls away.

Jax runs up, breathing hard. "What'd I miss? Had to hit the can before I had a serious incident. That last Gatorade . . . I swear my teeth were floating."

I shrug. "You didn't miss much. Alice might want to do some creepy photo stills for her movies."

Jax nods. "Sweet." He pauses. "Your stuff is pretty dope."

I don't look at him, but my cheeks redden a little, and I bite my lip to keep from making the chipmunk smile.

"Thanks," I mutter, in a voice that I hope is more I Get Compliments All the Time and less I'm Auditioning For the Squeaky Red Muppet on *Sesame Street*.

"No prob. See you tomorrow," he says, and walks away.

Molly has climbed into the same Volvo SUV as last time, which is once again parked on the farthest part of the driveway, like it's trying to avoid everyone else. Jax walks toward the minivan, which appears to be shaking slightly. When the door slides open, I hear sea shanties, played at a volume that is probably illegal, or should be, pouring out. Seriously, a galleon full of pirates would be quieter than that van. Jax shoots me a kill-me-now look before flashing me a peace sign and closing the door. As they drive by, I can hear a chorus of *"heave away, haul away"* through the closed windows. Jeez. Never again will I complain about my mom's National Public Radio obsession.

Andre has, as usual, slipped away without anyone noticing, so I'm solo. I glance around, still slightly creeped out by whatever went down with Erik. Was he going to confess? Threaten me? Kiss me? It was unclear, and frankly, the variety of options is seriously unnerving. But before I can even try to dissect whatever that was, my mom shows up.

"Am I on time?" she asks as I open the door. "I left work early today so I could be here early, but then I had to stop and pick up—"

"Mom, by your standards you *are* early," I say, settling into the passenger seat. "Thanks."

"I'm hoping maybe there was some resolution and you don't have to go back tomorrow."

I shake my head. "No, not really. We actually didn't get to have our second circle. Ms. Lewiston was tied up with something. So we'll be back tomorrow, I guess." I pause.

Mom glances at me. "What? What's going on? Were people awful?" Her mama-grizzly voice is threatening to make an appearance, so I pat her arm.

"No. Mom. Chill. Seriously, you need to chill."

"Well, I appreciate that, but honestly, Theo, this is not a joke. This was a hate crime. It was vandalism, and it was cruel. And then someone sabotaged your work in the darkroom the very next day! We need to get to the bottom of this. I'm sure it's terrible—"

I cut her off. "MOM. No. I'm actually wondering . . . I mean, is there any way to talk to Ms. Lewiston and tell her to forget it?"

My mom forgets to look at the light and is staring at me when the guy in the car behind us leans on his horn. I think of Alice.

As she drives, my mom keeps taking quick, frantic glances at me. "Theo. Why would you ask that?"

"Because it's stupid! Everyone's been really cool, and I

don't know who trashed my stuff, but even if it was one of them, I don't think they meant it, or—"

"They drew all over your work. They wrote slurs and graffiti on your—"

"I. KNOW." I don't mean to shout, but it comes out that way. I try to lower my voice. "I know, Mom. Obviously. But I think . . . I mean, I think we're over it. And I don't really want to know."

She looks over again, and her face is knotted up with worry. "Is this . . . Theo, is anyone threatening you, or asking you to drop this?"

"NO! Forget it. I just . . . I wanted to move on. To get past it, you know?" I lean my head against the window, and the icy glass feels good on my hot cheek. "I wanted to . . ."

I trail off without finishing my sentence. Because the truth is, I don't want to know who did it. I don't want to hear from Erik, or anyone else, for that matter. I want the whole thing to disappear. For the fun of the past few days to keep going, and for the six of us to actually maybe stay friends, or at least friendly, once school starts again next week. I don't want to know that one of them would do something like this.

"Oh, Theo," my mom says, and her voice sounds so sad that I want to do anything to make her stop talking.

"It's fine," I start, but she keeps going.

"Honey, I get it, I really do. But"—her voice catches a little—"if there's one thing I know, it's that you have to go through something to get to the other side. It's possible whoever damaged your work will have more to his or her story than we know, and hopefully you'll be able to hear and understand and forgive. But pretending it never happened . . . well, I'm here to tell you that rarely works."

I glance over at her, but she's looking straight ahead. Neither of us says anything about my dad, about all the travel he did, about how he used to call home every morning and night, no matter what the time difference was, then he'd only call at night, and then he'd miss a few nights because "his schedule was so nuts." He disappeared from our lives so slowly I'd barely noticed, but maybe my mom had.

"Yeah, I know," I say, and we're both quiet as I let my breath fog up the window.

CHAPTER 19

Well, That Sucks More Than I Expected It To

In a surreal turn of events, I'm actually excited to get to school in the morning. Partly to check the photos, sure, but also—and I kind of hate to admit it—to see everyone. But the excitement's also fighting gross, pit-of-the-stomach-churning nausea, worse than it's been since the first day. I know we're going to have our Justice Circle, and I don't know if I want to hear about whoever actually ruined my stuff. As we drive, I run through it in my mind. The options are depressing.

1) Molly: I know she's obsessed about not messing up, that her brother died recently, and that she's a serious sugar addict. Given that she would rather eat a bug than have a

teacher tell her she did something wrong,
I seriously cannot imagine her going all OG
on the student gallery.

2) Andre: I know he's got a secret famous
personality as a YouTube sensation death
metal drummer, but at school he's practically
invisible. He still swears he wasn't even
around when it happened. I know that kind
of sucks if he was there or not.

3) Erik: I don't know. He was the obvious
choice, but the more I get to know him, the
less I can figure it. I know he's actually as
intense about sports as is humanly possible,
but not in the trash-everything-else kind
of way his friends are. Then there's the fact
he seems to have a thing for Alice. He's also
so . . . nice. Normally when I say that, it's
kind of an insult (see also: boring, not funny),
but not this time. Erik's nice is just . . . you
know. *Nice.* Not at ALL like his butt-munch
teammates. He also has dyslexia and has to
work really hard in school, which I guess he
does, because he's not in special ed classes or
anything, even though it must suck to have

words and letters dance around and be hard
to read.

4) Jax: I know he's funnier than anyone else
and likes to make people laugh, but now I've
noticed he pulls back from anything nasty or
harsh. You can almost see him weighing his
next dig and holding off from the mean ones.
He's also kind of stressed out. . . . Not sure
why, but sometimes when he's not smiling,
he looks seriously miserable.

5) Alice: MVP of the Justice Circle, in my
opinion. The special effects makeup, the
general weirdness, the fact she is totally nice
to everyone . . . it's refreshing, in a strange
way. Also, whichever of her parents drives
that gold Lexus is seriously a piece of work.

Even though, thanks to Lewiston and her Justice Circle, I know way more about them, I still have no idea who
would have ruined my photographs. In fact, I have even *less*
of an idea than before. Before, I was pretty sure Erik did it
because he and his jockstrap friends find that sort of thing
amusing. Or possibly Jax, just to be a turd. I even thought
it was possible that Alice did it to be destructive and gothy

and weird. But now? Now I actually can't imagine any of them messing with my stuff.

And the fact that clearly one of them did makes me literally feel sick.

"Theo? You okay?" my mom says, and I startle.

We're in front of the school already.

"Oh, yeah. Sorry. Not enough coffee yet," I say, and she rolls her eyes.

"It's mostly decaf, you know that," she says, looking at my travel mug.

"Whatever. It's the placebo effect. Or something." But I pause before getting out of the car.

"I just . . . The more I get to know these guys, the weirder it seems that one of them trashed my stuff," I say finally.

My mom looks at me, her face soft.

"I thought this Justice Circle would prove that someone was, I don't know, an evil villain. Like out of *Scooby-Doo*, saying, 'I would have gotten away with it, if it weren't for those meddling kids.' But everyone seems cool. They all . . ." I swallow. "They all act like they like me." This is so literally pathetic that I cringe a little.

Mom bites her lip, and I'd bet my coffee she's trying not to cry. She's an easy cry, even on a good day. But she sounds normal. "You know, love, there are so many reasons things happen, both intentional and unintentional, that we can't possibly expect. Keep an open mind, okay? I think . . ." She clears her throat. "They probably *do* like you. Because you're awesome."

Now it's my turn to roll my eyes, which I do while opening the door. "Please. You're an adult. You, like, legally *have* to say that."

"I do not," she says, lowering the window as I shut the door. "There are plenty of kids I think are little trolls and probably aren't particularly well liked. You happen not to be one of them." She blows me a kiss.

I wave. "Thanks, I guess," I say. "And maybe you shouldn't say that to the kids at your library—"

"Oh, quiet," she says. "I'm always nice, even to the little trolls! That's what grown-ups do!" And with that wisdom, she's gone.

As I head toward the door, I nearly step on a phone lying on the pavement. I can't help feeling a little bit smug. The only advantage of being one of the rare kids in middle school without a smartphone is that I don't have to worry about losing a six-hundred-dollar toy the size of a candy bar. When I bend down to grab it, the thing lights up with around ten texts in a row, the background screen a photo of a basketball whooshing into a net. Erik's phone, I have to assume. And apparently, he dropped it in the middle of a group chat.

Of course I read it, because I'm nosy like that.

I wish I hadn't.

DreamTeam4EVA

Kev: You loving school a little too much

Shaun: Truth

Kev: Remember your teammates come first right? States this year bro.

Jude: What's even your issue? All you got to do is shut up

Shaun: Coach thinks your wack, btw. He's pissed.

Jude: But we love you man

Jude: Where are you?

Jude: Yo you ghosting? WTH?

Kev: Think about it. Kids a puke anyway so who cares

Kev: Weeks almost over. No proof means it all goes away

Oh.

So that's that. It should be my moment of vindication, because—YAY ME!—I was right all along. Erik and his trash chunk friends had it out for me. So that's a relief, right? Because it means my instincts are totally on.

I don't feel relieved. At all. Actually, I feel like I might throw up. I breathe deep, head between my knees, until it passes.

There. I'm fine.

I think back to our conversation outside the gym and have an immediate desire to scrub my brain with bleach so that all the laughing and dude-punches are obliterated. Obviously, I was wrong—hilariously wrong—to imagine Erik was having fun, was actually a decent human being. Which is fine. I was expecting that, wasn't I?

I bite down hard on the inside of my cheek and blink.

Force myself to think about summer vacation, about switching schools, about getting out of here and never ever looking back.

When I'm sure I can breathe without doing anything pathetic or stupid, I make my feet move toward room 201. As I walk, I relax my jaw and shoulders, try to smooth out my eyebrows. Try to seem normal.

They don't need to know anything. Because truth? Why would I care that Erik is *exactly* what he's always seemed to be: a total jockstrap? I don't care. And even the rest of them . . . Maybe they knew the truth all along, maybe not. Hard to believe they're *all* clueless about what went down. They can stay in this stupid Justice Circle or get suspended or rat him out if they're feeling brave. They're not my friends, and they're not my problem.

I drop the phone in the hallway, not particularly caring whether the screen shatters. Erik can retrace his steps and find it. Or not. Add that to the list of things that aren't my problem.

As my feet move down the hall, I repeat a mantra in my head along with the rhythm of my footsteps: *Don't care don't care don't care don't care . . .*

But the nauseated, sweaty feeling cramping my stomach tells me otherwise.

Still, when I get to the door, I pause, make my face and shoulders relax, and do everything I can to look normal walking in. I force myself to think about the pinhole cameras. This seventeen-hour exposure is something I've never tried before, and my mind keeps up a lively game of Ping-Pong: Side One: *Think about the photos, Theo. These are going to be the best photos you've ever taken.* Side Two: *The photos will be garbage and everyone in there is garbage and the best thing to do is walk away.* I try not to keep score.

But when I go in, I don't remember to make my face look casual and calm.

Because everyone looks gutted. I stand in the doorway, waiting for someone to tell me what's going on. But instead, no one looks at me and everyone falls silent.

"What?" I say finally. "What happened?"

It's Alice, brave, weird Alice, who finally turns and walks over to me. Vaguely I notice she has what looks like rope burn around her neck.

"The cameras. They're . . . well." She gestures around the room. The closet door is shut and the cameras are nowhere to be seen.

"They're gone. Only the candle one is still there, and someone moved it."

I look around. She's right. There's no sign of the careful setups we did yesterday, no sign of the quote or even the Matchbox car.

"Theo," Ms. Lewiston starts saying, but I put my hand up to stop her. She steps forward and puts a hand on my shoulder. I want to shrug it off, want to run out of the room, but my body has gone into lockdown mode. This makes no sense. There must be a reason . . . right? Did Erik come back in and ruin them? But why? Everyone was really into it, weren't they? Or were they faking it? Was this whole thing a big joke?

I find my legs. "I gotta go. Bathroom," I mumble, and turn and move toward the door.

"Theo, wait! Let's get into our circle and talk—" Ms. Lewiston starts, but I'm gone.

And I don't plan on coming back.

CHAPTER 20

Day Four Assessments

Date: Feb. 21

Name: *Molly Claremont*

What happened and what were you thinking at the time of the incident?

Poor Theo. Someone messed with his photos again. Although this time I'd say whoever it was messed with all of us, because we all worked on this.

What have you thought about since?

I can't help wondering WHO? I mean, we've been hanging out all week, and everyone actually has been pretty nice, and, you know, normal. But someone was faking it. Someone's even better at faking it than I am, because I totally believed them.

What about this has been hardest for you?
I guess I wasn't expecting to care so much.

What do you think needs to be done to make things as right as possible?
We NEED to get to the bottom of this. It's not just about Theo anymore. It's about all of us.

Is there anything at all you'd like to share confidentially with Ms. Lewiston?
It makes no sense. I mean, there is NO WAY that the people who vandalized the gallery were able to get in and do this to the cameras. It just doesn't make sense.

Name: Andre Hall

What happened and what were you thinking at the time of the incident?
Someone messed up Theo's stuff AGAIN. I was actually pretty excited to see how the photos

were going to turn out, so I have to say, it feels like whoever did it is messing with me now too.

What have you thought about since?
I guess I thought we were friends, but it's probably good to be reminded that we're not before school starts back up again.

What about this has been hardest for you?
Just another day being Andre.

What do you think needs to be done to make things as right as possible?
I wish we could figure this out so that the rest of us could move on.

Is there anything at all you'd like to share confidentially with Ms. Lewiston?
Makes you wonder if there's any point to this at all, doesn't it?

Name: Erik Estrale

What happened and what were you thinking at the time of the incident?

This is dirty play . . . a total foul if I ever saw one. Who does this to their own teammate? And this Justice Circle is kind of like a team. I really don't get how this happened. ~~How could they even~~

What have you thought about since?

I'm mad. Like, really mad. I shouldn't say this, but I'm tempted to invite someone out for a little one-on-one, you know?

What about this has been hardest for you?

We all worked on these cameras! This isn't just Theo. This is about me, and all of us.

What do you think needs to be done to make things as right as possible?

We're going to need to catch the perps, and then I recommend suicides and wind sprints for an HOUR. See how they feel about that.

Is there anything at all you'd like to share confidentially with Ms. Lewiston?

~~I need to~~

~~Something hap~~

Can I talk to you in private?

Name: Alice Shu

What happened and what were you thinking at the time of the incident?

I was the first into the classroom today, because my dad dropped me off a half hour early. I was excited to see the photographs, but I wasn't going to touch the cameras, because I wasn't sure exactly how Theo planned to finish the shots. But when I got there they were gone. I was horrified, honestly. I also wondered if whoever did it was lurking in the classroom, so I immediately checked the closet and under the teacher's desk. (No one was hiding.)

What have you thought about since?

I guess there's no way to really know someone, even if you think you do.

What about this has been hardest for you?
Mostly I'm sad for Theo, but I'm also sorry that we probably won't all be friends anymore.

What do you think needs to be done to make things as right as possible?
Well, it wasn't me. Probably we need some kind of entrapment scheme to see if we can figure out who did it. Like, Theo should stay late, and when he's all alone and hanging up some photographs, we'll hide and see who comes along to sabotage them.

Is there anything at all you'd like to share confidentially with Ms. Lewiston?
I've been thinking a lot about horror movies and how there are usually false clues to lead you away from the killer, who then uses the opportunity to do something even worse. I'm scared for Theo. Although maybe it's because I watched a super-terrifying Korean horror movie last night.

Name: Jax Fletcher

What happened and what were you thinking at the time of the incident?

This is INSANE. Who the heck would mess with Theo again? Here? Now? It makes no sense.

What have you thought about since?

Honestly, I'm side-eyeing everyone here, wondering what's up. Because I thought we were all cool. But obviously I was wrong.

What about this has been hardest for you?

I just wanted to get out of here. Looked like we were on track for a hot minute, but now that's done. We're here all week.

What do you think needs to be done to make things as right as possible?

I have NO idea. Who'd trash his stuff <u>again</u>??

Is there anything at all you'd like to share confidentially with Ms. Lewiston?

I'm NOT saying I did anything, because I didn't. But I'm curious—what's going to happen when you find out who it was?

CHAPTER 21

Ugly-Crying by the Urinals
Is Exactly as Fun as It Sounds

I stay in the bathroom for at least thirty minutes. Luckily, I'm alone at first, because I can't help it: I let loose with snort-roar-cry noises like some kind of beast. I even punch the paper towel roll, which makes my hand sting like it's been swarmed by fire ants and also knocks the thing loose from the wall, so the paper towels roll everywhere.

I look at the mess and sigh. By the time I'm done picking them up and rerolling them, I'm calmer. But the Snort-RoarCry beast is resting, not gone. My chest is tight, and I'm sweaty and so, so angry.

Then comes the parade.

Erik shows up first, which is just perfect. There is literally no one else on this earth I want to see less right now. He says he's there to bring me back to the circle, talking all about pulling together and handling it like a team, but

I refuse to even look at him. Part of me wants to scream at him and tell him that I'll be letting Lewiston and Davis know that his adorable little teammates are all but outing him on his phone, but I can't even make myself care. Maybe Lewiston will figure it out on her own, but she's not hearing it from me.

He keeps babbling. After I ignore him for ten minutes, he leaves. Then Jax comes in, and he's a little harder to deal with. First of all, he squats down and peers at me from under the stall door.

"Dude, you aren't, like, making use of your time in there or anything, right? 'Cause that would be seriously awkward for both of us."

I grunt. My pants are on, obviously, and I've managed to perch on the toilet paper holder with my feet on the toilet. It's uncomfortable, but somehow squatting on the can was too pathetic even for me.

Jax sighs with relief. "Cool. That was a risk, right there. Didn't know what I'd be staring up into."

I look away. The sight of Jax's head half resting on the germ-covered bathroom floor is not the kind of thing that lifts the spirits.

"Dude, I know this is bad, but come on. Let's go back and talk to Lewiston and see if she can shake something loose. I mean, someone's gonna have to admit it, or at least look shifty and stuff." He sighs. "Man, this is one nasty floor. I'm coming in." With that he slithers under the door and just like that he's standing in front of me.

As brutally bad as this morning has been, this is even worse. I jump down in shock and am now pressed within six inches of Jax, his flat brim almost knocking me in the nose as I try to get by him.

"Do. You. MIND?" I ask, pushing toward the stall door.

But he leans against it. "Hold your fire, bro. I just want you to know. I got your back. We'll figure out who did this."

I want to get mad at him, or ignore him, or something, but it turns out I don't have the energy. After all that screaming and punching the paper towels, I'm now exhausted deep down to my bones. I want to go to sleep and wake up when seventh grade is over. I climb back onto the toilet paper roll.

"Go. Away," I say. "I don't care anymore." I let my hair fall down around my face and ignore him until he finally unlocks the stall and walks out.

"If Lewiston's handing out Starburst, I'll bring some in," he says as he leaves. "Though you gotta wash your hands. That's just unsanitary."

I stay silent, and he heads out, the soft *clack* of the door letting me know I'm alone again. I leave the stall door open and stare at the rust-colored stains on the floor. The hurt is far away, almost numb. Part of me feels like I'm watching myself from above, watching the loser kid, the bullied kid, hiding out in the bathroom, sniveling and pathetic and sad. It feels so removed from me that it almost doesn't hurt, but there's a whisper, a hint of what's to come, like when you slam something on your toe and there's a second of emptiness before the red-hot pain crashes in. I know it's waiting for me.

A few minutes later Andre comes in, but he doesn't even try very hard. He takes one look at me, sitting on the toilet paper holder, and pauses by the sink.

"Can I get you anything?" His voice is quiet, as always, but he sounds more . . . there. Like he's actually present.

I glance at him, then back down. "No. Thanks, though."

"No problem. You want to maybe come out, circle up with us? Lewiston is really upset. She's trying to get some answers."

I look up. "Is anyone admitting to anything?"

Andre's worried face answers for him. Yeah. I didn't think so.

I shake my head. "You go ahead. I'm fine."

Andre stays a few more seconds. "Okay." He starts to walk out.

"Hey. Theo?" he says, one hand on the door.

I give a barely audible grunt.

"Just . . . for what it's worth, I didn't do it. I think your photos are pretty dope. And, well, don't know if you'll want to, but I talked about your work with the band, and we'd hire you to take some stills. If you're interested."

I don't say anything, and Andre shuffles his feet a little. Finally he says, "Yeah, didn't figure it'd be something you'd want. That's cool."

I get an uncomfortable clench in my stomach at how small his voice sounds. I close my eyes for a second, then open them again, planning to try to thank him for even caring enough about my photos to ask.

But he's gone, silent as usual.

It's not until Alice comes into the boys' room that I actually wrap up my pity party and get out of there.

I've moved from the toilet paper holder to the toilet itself, with my head buried in my arms, when the door flies open for the fourth time. Alice comes in at a trot, almost slamming into the urinals on the wall.

"Oh, hey! I guess I never actually thought about these! You know, they look sort of creepy, all lined up like that. Like upright coffins." She peers closer. "WOW. They smell pretty bad, though." She steps back. "Definitely would need some preparation before shooting anything in here."

I've barely moved, though there's something horribly embarrassing about sitting on a toilet in the presence of a girl. Even Alice.

"You're not pooping, right?" she says, coming toward the stalls. My door is still slightly ajar, and she hesitates for a second. "Because I totally want to respect your privacy if you are."

I kick at the door so it closes, then swings wider. "No. I'm not pooping," I say, and my voice sounds weird and flat, even to me.

"Good." She moves to the stall next to me. "So, these look pretty much the same as the girls' room. Different graffiti, though." She's silent for a minute.

I bend down to look at her feet. They're planted like she's sitting.

"I actually really do have to pee," she says. "So if you don't mind turning the water on in one of the sinks that would be really helpful. I get pee shy."

I take a deep breath. My eyes are still red and sticky, and I have that gross embarrassed, nauseated feeling in my stomach, but ... well, Alice. Also my butt is getting kind of sore.

I get up and go to the sink, turning on the faucet.

"Thank you!" Alice calls from inside her thankfully

closed and locked stall. "Does that ever happen to you? If it's really quiet, you can't pee? My sister used to sing me the pee song to help. But now she's at college."

I don't even know where to start. "What's the pee song?" I ask finally. I don't want it to get too quiet, in case Alice slows midstream.

"Well, you know, it was really the *Star Wars* theme, sung with the word *pee*. Like *PEE Pee, peepeepee PEE Pee . . .*" She trails off.

"Done!" she announces, and comes out, fixing her tights. "Thank you. Seriously." She stands next to me at the sink and washes her hands.

I turn and look at the mirror, at our two reflections. Her face looks totally normal today, which is a little disappointing. Our eyes meet in the mirror, and she grins.

"Check it," she says, pointing to the back of her head.

I look and try not to scream. She's created a kind of Voldemort-coming-out-of-Quirrell's-head situation, except that instead of a Dark Lord, there's some reptilian *thing* erupting from her skull.

"Wow. That's . . . wow."

I seem to have lost my verbal skills. But she beams.

"I *know*," she responds. "It's my *pièce de résistance*! I was so excited for today!" She sighs.

A weird silence falls. I want to tell her to save her breath and go back and circle up with the others, but at the same time I'm glad she's here. I had gone from Beast anger to more basic sad-and-bored. Truth? I don't know how much longer I could have hung out on that toilet.

"So," she says. "Everyone's freaking out, kind of." She reports this in her usual cheerful, almost singsongy voice.

I give a half shrug/half nod. I don't want to say what I'm thinking, which is, in a nutshell, GOOD. I HOPE THEY'RE ALL CRYING INTO THEIR STARBURSTS.

But Alice goes on. "You know, I make movies, so I write a lot of stories, and I'm also pretty good at observing people." She pauses. "Usually people don't really talk to me much, so it's easy to observe."

I can't help glancing up at this. Her voice is still bright, but a little of my self-righteous anger slithers away. It can't be easy to be Alice, no matter how fun she makes it look.

"Anyway," she says, after a pause, "I bring that up because I've been observing the four other people in the room, and honestly, Theo, I don't think any of them did it." She looks at me, and her dark eyes are sympathetic. "I don't know what to say. But everyone seems seriously confused."

I blink and grab the shreds of my anger. I'd rather be pissed and surly than pathetic. "Whatever, Alice. One of them DID do it, though. And I'm pretty sure I know who.

Maybe the others know, and maybe they don't. I have no idea. For all I know, they're covering up for each other."

She shakes her head, her hair swinging out of her bun. "Oops! I need to keep the hair out of Slinky back there!" she says, grabbing it and pinning it all up. "Can you check if any is . . . you know . . . sticking?"

She turns, and I'm confronted with the reptile bursting out of her skull. Slinky? Seriously? Freaking ALICE.

I try not to back up. "It's uh . . . it's fine, I think."

She whips back around so that instead of blood and scales, I'm confronted with her giant smile. "Thank you!" she chirps. "Anyway, I don't think they're covering. I told you. I'm a keen observer of humankind. They're perplexed."

I fold my arms across my chest. "Perplexed." It's not a question.

She nods. "Yes. Flummoxed. Confused. Discombobulated. Shocked. You get the idea. They're not acting like people with something to hide."

"But they are! Someone knows something. Obviously. Or else we wouldn't be here in the first place!" Oh good. Just like that the anger is back, and poor Alice is right in the kill zone. "I don't care how good you are at observing people! Because what I'm good at is facts. And the fact here is that this is the third time my stuff's been trashed, and someone in our little Justice Club has it in for me."

"But if you'd—" she starts, but I'm done.

"WHY SHOULD I?" I yell. And the shouting-raging-monster-me is there, ready to attack. Alice winces and moves away. But I'm too far gone to care. "GIVE ME ONE. GOOD. REASON! What do I owe you, or the rest of them, to go out there and keep ruining my vacation pretending we're all being brave and honest and opening up and becoming BFFs. Tell me! WHY?"

Alice has backed up to the door, and she's now holding it open, waiting. I just stare.

"Because we're all here too. And some of us are innocent. You're not the only victim here," she says softly. "You're not the only one who matters. And I know you're a good enough person to care about that."

I open my mouth, then close it again. I try again to grab my self-pity, but instead, I see Andre's face, when he talked about his band practicing without him, and even Molly, whose hands still shake when we're supposed to be sharing in circle.

We stand there for a few seconds, or maybe longer. My shoulders drop, and I can actually feel my heartbeat slow. Finally I nod. "Yeah. Okay," I say, and head for the door.

As we leave, we nearly bang into Jax, who is coming in at a run. "You all good?" he asks as he rounds the corner.

"Glad you're coming out, but, dude, I gotta go. Like, NOW. You probably wanna dip."

Alice and I look at each other, and I make my eyes big. She nods vigorously. "Yeah, let's get out of here," she says, and we slam the door as Jax flies into a stall behind us.

Alice glances at me as we walk back to the classroom. "That was a kind of close call," she says.

All I can do is laugh. But by the time I get back to the room, I don't feel like laughing anymore.

CHAPTER 22

Well, That Escalated Quickly

When we walk in, everyone freezes, old-school-Western-style. I almost expect someone to draw a pistol or something. But instead, Ms. Lewiston says, "Oh, Theo, I'm glad you came back."

I shrug.

"When Jax comes in from the bathroom, we're going to circle up and talk about this. And, people"—here she looks at each of us in turn—"it's time to open up. It's time to step up. It's time."

As usual, we're in our circle, with the piece of fabric on the floor and the birch talking stick next to it. Even the pathetic drugstore fake candle is back, which fuels my rage all over again.

Andre looks down at his desk. Molly glares at something

behind Ms. Lewiston's head. Erik looks at her like she's giving very intricate instructions in Swahili on crocheting. He doesn't even have the brains to look guilty. And Alice carefully pokes behind her head to make sure Slinky is still in place.

I have exactly zero hopes for this entire thing.

Jax bounces in and pulls his chair into place (with the obligatory *screeeeeeeeeech* and Molly's Why Me, Lord face).

"Okay, so we're doing this," Ms. Lewiston says once Jax sits. "Who wants to start? We can begin by each saying how we feel right now. And I want to remind you: honesty."

She hands me the talking stick, and I take it but let it fall on the desk.

"Theo?" she says, and her voice is normal, but there's something in the way she says those two syllables, like she wants to push me and protect me at the same time.

I sigh. Pick up the stick. Flick it between my fingers. "Well, I feel . . ." I pause. Look up. Molly's eyes are on me, and she's scowling. I scowl back. "I'm mad. Like, seriously epically NOT HAPPY. Because this makes three times. Three times someone has bothered to ruin something I made. So let's review, shall we? First of all, at the gallery, the five of you were *there*, okay? You were RIGHT THERE. And you're all saying you saw nothing, did nothing, know nothing. And the next day, someone went into the dark-room and ruined my long-exposure cameras. And again, no one knows anything. And now this. Now, with only the six of us in the building, it happened again. So yeah, *while* it's technically *possible* I guess, through some kind of time-space continuum rip, that someone else vandalized the gallery and NOBODY SAW ANYTHING AT ALL, there's no way anyone else messed with these pinhole cameras. So that means this whole week, all the talking, and yoga-ball soccer, and candy"—OOPS. I feel rather than see Jax jerk in the seat next to me like something stung him. Oh well—"was total bull. At least for someone. And that just really, really . . ." My voice trails off.

"Stinks." This is Alice, filling in the word.

Ms. Lewiston doesn't reprimand Alice for talking without the talking stick. She nods.

"Thanks, Theo. Anger seems pretty reasonable right now. But maybe you're feeling other things too?"

I shake my head, not in disagreement, but because I'm done talking for now. "Who's next?" I ask, holding up the stick.

"I'll take it," Alice says, and as I pass it to her across the circle, she gives my hand a small squeeze.

"I can tell you, I feel betrayed, I guess," she says, lean-ing back in her seat and speaking in the same cheerful voice as usual. "I feel like, for a little while at least, I had friends, the way normal people do. Like we might say hi to each other, or ask each other how our weekend was. And now I guess I feel like someone here who would trick Theo into thinking they were friends, and that they cared about the cameras, then would trash them . . . well. I guess someone who would do that wouldn't really be my friend after all."

There's silence after this, and everyone looks at their desks. Then Erik slams his hand down and looks up, straight at Alice. Except her head is bowed, so he's actually looking more at Slinky. He does a double take, then says, with the kind of tone I associate with battlefield speeches, "I'll still say hi to you! And ask about your weekend!" His face is quite red.

Jax raises one eyebrow, but no one says anything.

Alice looks at Erik for several seconds before smiling. "Thanks" is all she says. But Erik looks satisfied.

It crosses my mind to wonder if he's an actual sociopath. Like, someone who actually doesn't realize that destroying someone's work and also pretending to be their friend is all kinds of messed up. But he can play his Good Boy Scout role for Alice all he wants. I'm not buying it.

"Who's next?" she asks, holding out the stick.

Molly grabs it. Her hands are trembling again. "I'll go,"

she says. "I'll tell you how I feel. I'm scared. I mean, I can't be suspended. I can't. I just can't! My parents . . . I told them this whole week was a special intensive pre-algebra prep course, which is fine, but if I have to explain . . ." She stops talking.

Ms. Lewiston looks concerned. "But a letter went home, Molly. They signed—"

"*I* signed it, okay? I sign everything that gets sent home! And I can't get in trouble over this. Don't you get it?" Molly's scarlet now, holding on to her ponytail like she wants to pull it out of her head.

Jax leans forward. "Girl, what is your *problem*? You're every parent's dream and you know it! What, you think if you do one thing wrong, they're going to lose it? Try living in my shoes for a week and see how you like it! 'Jax was disruptive in science!' 'Jax needs to concentrate more in math!' 'Unfortunately, Jax's last quiz shows no improvement.' Man! You worry about messing up once like it would be the end of the world!"

Ms. Lewiston turns to him. "Jax, first of all, it's not your turn to speak. And second, I want you to think about what it feels like to have your words invalidated like that. To be told 'you shouldn't feel that way.' Because that's what you told Molly. She's—"

"That's not what I said!" Jax yells, jumping up.

"That's exactly what you said! And you know NOTH-ING about my life, got it?" Molly yells back. She stands up, pushing her chair so that it falls over with a giant CRASH.

Alice squeaks.

"My parents can't handle ANYTHING. Okay? My brother *died* this summer, and they—they can barely get out of bed in the morning. They don't cook, they don't shop, they don't check homework, they don't pay bills. I'm keeping everything going for me and my sister and We. Are. FINE. But they're so useless they might as well have died too!"

With that she shoves past Ms. Lewiston, who's standing up, and pushes Jax with all her strength. He gives a cry of alarm and, off balance, falls over, crashing into his chair.

Molly sobs and rushes toward the door. As she pushes it open, Ms. Davis must be pulling it from the other side, because the door flies open, and Molly smashes into Davis at full speed.

"OOOF!" Ms. Davis grunts, crashing into the wall. "*What* is going on here?"

But Molly Claremont, paragon of Shipton excellence, has broken. "GO TO HELL!" she shrieks, and dashes down the hall.

The only sound is the crashing of her footsteps.

From the floor, Jax groans a little. "Dude. I hit my head,

I think." He lifts his hand away from the back of his head, and sure enough, there's blood on his hand.

"Ooooh, that looks sick," Alice whispers, but one look at Davis and she shuts up with a squeak.

"Mr. Fletcher. To the office. Immediately. And, Ms. Lewiston"—here Davis pulls herself up like an X-Men villain and glares—"come with me."

CHAPTER 23

People Say Lots of Things but None of Them Answers the Question

The funny part is that when I sat in the bathroom stall surrounded by graffiti and the unrelenting stank of classmates who don't even try to aim, I thought things were bad. And yet, in the fifteen minutes since I came out, we've gone nuclear. Leaving aside the whole someone-hates-me-and-wants-to-ruin-my-stuff factor, now:

1) Davis is raging, and if that whole "staff cuts" threat from before is true, Ms. Lewiston could lose her job.
2) Molly's life is legit falling apart and she's freaking out.
3) Jax has a bleeding head wound (a real one, not an Alice-created one).

Truth? Somewhere deep inside, I'm actually frustrated that everything's blown up like this, because it means I'm not even the one people feel sorry for anymore. I mean, *I* can't even feel all that sorry for myself, which is a serious buzzkill.

Andre, Erik, Alice, and I stare at each other.

"Well, does anyone want this?" Alice asks, holding up the talking stick.

Andre and I silently shake our heads. Erik stares at it for long seconds, as though trying to set it on fire with his mind. (Although maybe it's just me who used to try doing that. Never worked.)

Finally Erik grabs the stick. "I want it," he says. "Because I have something to say."

I lean back in my chair and cross my arms. Here we go. But the real question is: Will he threaten us to keep quiet, or does he figure that none of us losers is even worth the effort? I try to look like I don't care, but the stabby stomach pains are back, and I want to curl up in a ball. I try to remind myself that this is vindication . . . that I knew it was him all along. But instead, there's a deep gut-churning ache. Part of me, I realize, still wants to be wrong.

Erik looks past me, right at Andre. "I want to say I'm sorry," he says. "I've been thinking about the fact that you said you were in the bathroom, not in the gallery, and none of us even noticed you. That's just . . . not right. I mean, it was a small group, and you're . . . you're like . . ." He's quiet for a second, looking puzzled.

"One-sixth of us," Alice chirps.

Erik shoots her a grateful look. "Yeah. Exactly. It's not cool that we didn't even notice you."

Andre nods slowly. "Thanks, man. I appreciate that."

Erik nods too. We all sit in silence, nodding at each other like those old-school bobbleheads. I lean back and exhale. I don't know what to do with the relief that makes my arms and back floppy. I close my eyes for a second, wishing this whole thing were over and I could move on to important things, like looking up new darkroom techniques on YouTube or clearing a massive deuce from Otis's litter box. Anything other than this.

Alice speaks up. "I knew you weren't there. But I thought it would be more fun if you came this week."

We all spin to look at her. She looks back, her cheeks a little pinker than usual. "I just . . . well, we have LA and math together, and you're so quiet I wondered if you had a secret. Like, a secret persona. I thought it would be interesting to get to know you . . ." She stops talking and looks at Andre. "Well. Sorry. I guess I want to apologize."

Andre looks stunned. "You what?" he asks, and his voice is squeaky-toy-high at the end. "Wait, are you serious?"

It should be noted that Andre's voice is now literally the loudest I've ever heard. I wonder if he's going to go full death-metal-crazy on Alice, which is somewhat exciting, somewhat terrifying to imagine.

But Erik, apparently, is too committed to his freakishly-fake-nice-guy routine to leave it hanging.

"Well, I'm seriously glad you're here, even though it was a bad call," he says. "I mean, otherwise I don't think I'd ever have known about your drumming, or your sick band, or anything. And now I'm following you on YouTube and Instagram, so you've got fifty thousand and one followers!"

Andre stares for a second, then laughs, which I think shows that he's a seriously decent human being. He shakes his head. "Alice, you're a trip. Well, at least you noticed me, so that's cool." He laughs again. "We're good."

We lapse back into silence. The gut churn starts all over again.

I want Erik—and everyone else—to tell the truth. I want to know if they're all lying, all faking everything I'm seeing and hearing. But at the same time, I don't want to know. If I don't know for sure, I don't have to deal with it. I look away from them, watching the door, waiting for Ms. Lewiston to come back, waiting for Molly to come back, even waiting for Jax to come back and reassure us he doesn't have a concussion or anything.

Finally the door swings open and Molly walks in. Her face is blotchy, half red, half pale, and her careful braid is frizzed out. But otherwise, she looks normal.

Luckily, we have Alice, who will always choose awkward comments over awkward silence. She jumps up. "You're back! I was worried about you but had a feeling you didn't want company. You seem like someone who would rather cry alone." She walks over to Molly and puts her arms around her. "But that doesn't mean I can't hug you, right?"

Molly stands there, her arms pinned to her sides, while Alice hugs her. Molly's face is frighteningly close to Slinky, but somehow her expression is empty of its usual Someone Hand Me a Vat of Hand Sanitizer look. It's empty of everything, really, but she closes her eyes for a second and lets herself be hugged.

Alice lets go. "Here," she says, leading Molly back to her chair, which someone has picked up. "I brought you something."

Alice opens her backpack, and Andre, Erik, and I all peer forward, curious. Molly leans back slightly. I can't totally blame her. With Alice, there's no knowing what might come out of there. Could be an origami crane, could be a pickled shark in a jar. As we all learned the hard way.

But Alice pulls out a small wax-paper envelope. "Here. I made these last night."

Molly opens the bag and gasps. "You made this for me?"

She holds it up so we can all see. It's a cookie, but that doesn't really do it justice, because it looks like it was decorated with lace and cobwebs and snowflakes. It's the most intricate thing I've ever seen.

Alice shrugs. "Well, I thought you'd like it, since you're kind of into sugar. I love to bake. Or, really, to decorate baking. It's not that different from special effects, though I use less blood."

Molly blinks, and for a minute her empty expression looks so impossibly sad that I have to look away. But she smiles at Alice, a real smile, and her blotches fade a little.

"It looks amazing," she says. "But I can't eat it. I want to save it forever!"

"It'll mold or something," Alice says with a shrug. "So you should probably eat it."

"You could take a picture!" Erik says, then claps his hand over his mouth, his eyes huge. It would have been funny—like a kid who dropped an f-bomb at the Thanksgiving table—except that it jackhammers home that there are secrets and lies all over the place.

There's another awkward silence that even Alice doesn't try to break.

Finally I speak up. For this moment, at least, I feel like I have nothing left to lose.

"Seriously, you guys, it's okay. But . . . can you tell me the truth? I don't even care anymore." I pause and sigh. "Okay, I care, but . . . whatever. I just want to move on. So, you know. If you can tell me anything . . ." I let the words trail off and look at them, starting with Erik, then looking around the room.

No one is looking at me. No one answers.

The only sound in the room is the soft crunch of Molly eating.

CHAPTER 24

When Davis Wins, the Smell of Burning Sulfur and Children's Tears Fill the Air. . . . Fun Times.

Ms. Lewiston doesn't come back. Instead, Ms. Davis walks in, her shoes slamming into the floor like she's trying to hammer nails.

She levels us all with a stare and says, "I think it's *abundantly* clear that this 'Justice Club'"—and here she makes totally annoying finger quotes—"is not going to yield satisfactory answers. Theo, am I right that your work has been tampered with again? In this classroom? With only your so-called partners in justice knowledgeable about its existence?"

I close my eyes for a second, wishing for a TARDIS, or a wormhole, or even a stomach flu . . . anything that would get me out of this room. When I open them, Alice, Andre, Erik, and Molly are all staring at me. I lower my gaze and shrug.

Ms. Davis stomps forward until her sensible skirt-and-jacket combo are inches from me. I don't look up.

"Mr. Gustav. Please. I don't know about you, but I would like answers here, and that means starting now, with your own voice. Did you or did you not have work ruined again last night?"

I swallow hard. It's not like I'm going to lie. Why would I? The cameras are gone, and someone here must have done it, unless there's some secret photography-hating spy ninja-ing around the school and popping out when everything's dark and quiet. This seems like an unlikely scenario.

"Yeah," I say finally. "I guess. I mean, we don't know who did it, but—"

Ms. Davis bulldozes right over me, and honesty compels me to admit I don't really have anything useful to add, anyway. I mean, the cameras were trashed. Period.

"So," Ms. Davis says, looking around at everyone else. "It seems that Ms. Lewiston's plan for openness and caring hasn't quite panned out. Your time and mine has been wasted, and for what? For some fantasy version of education. Now here we are, with one day left of vacation, and we are no closer to the truth, are we?"

No one answers, which seems wise. Ms. Davis already looks way too delighted that this has gone so badly off course.

"Now that we're done playing at 'alternative' solutions, we will proceed to the point where we should have started in the first place. Theo, you are free to leave today and not return until school starts on Monday. You were victimized here and bear no responsibility. The rest of you will come back tomorrow and sit in detention. *Real* detention. Ms. Lewiston can sit with you, but you will be in *my* office, and following my rules. If no one confesses, you will *all* be suspended for three days, beginning on Monday. I hope for your sakes that someone manages to tell the truth, or you will all be considered guilty. And your coaches, teachers, and parents will of course be informed."

Alice sneezes twice, and Ms. Davis looks at her suspiciously but says nothing. Instead, she looks back at me.

"I'm sorry, Theo, that you were not only victimized yet again, but also forced to lose your vacation to this obviously unsuccessful effort. I'm afraid Ms. Lewiston has all kinds of excuses and stories that allow perpetrators to feel entitled to the damage they cause. Again, it's a real pity that you were caught up in this. It's almost like you were a victim all over again. I *am* sorry."

It should be noted that Ms. Davis does not look sorry. She looks freaking delighted, and her mouth seems to savor the word *victim* a little more than a normal person's would. The sight of her barely contained glee makes my fist clench.

"I'm actually fine with what Ms. Lewiston did," I say, and I make myself look around the room. "Even if we didn't find out who did it, I think she's right. I think there's probably more to the story than I know, and I'm glad we were all here. I mean, I definitely got to know my classmates better."

My face flames as I say this, but watching the smirk fall off Ms. Davis's face is almost worth it. Still, if I thought my little speech was going to rally the troops, I was destined to be horribly disappointed. No one stands up in support, or tearfully confesses to vandalizing my work, for that matter. Alice appears to have lost all interest in the conversation and is squinting at something outside the window and murmuring under her breath. The others look down at the floor.

I let my hair fall over my face. Whatever. It's not like I expected them to suddenly step up and admit the truth. No matter what I said—and let's be honest, I mostly said it to mess with Ms. Davis—these guys might have stories and secrets of their own, but they're still keeping to their proper place in the food chain of Shipton Middle School. They matter, and they're not about to screw with that for me. I want to be angry again, but instead, all that's left is a hollow gut-punch emptiness. This train wreck of an ending confirms what I guess I knew: people can't help but disappoint you, no matter what.

Ms. Davis makes a horse-snort sound and yammers on about effective discipline and zero tolerance (of course) until finally she winds down.

"Do you have anything you want to say to Theo before we leave?" she asks.

I look up for a second, but no one meets my eyes. Molly and Erik are staring at the floor, no doubt thinking about how much it will suck to tell their parents that they're going to be suspended after this whole thing. Andre looks at Alice like he's expecting her to speak up for him, but she's staring out the window and doesn't say anything. After a few seconds, Andre stares down at his lap and stays silent.

"Fine." Ms. Davis sounds downright triumphant, which makes me feel even more of that post-puking hollow queasiness. "Theo, you are free to wait in here or in the lobby until pickup," she says. "And I want you to know, this kind of hate, this bullying, this blatant unkindness to make a student feel unwelcome ... well, it has no place in our school. We will continue to have ZERO TOLERANCE for this behavior." She takes a long, theatrical look at her watch. "And as soon as Ms. Lewiston returns to chaperone you, I will go prepare my office to serve as a detention room. Then she will escort you down there."

With that she flaps her hands at everyone, telling them

to pack up at once and asking for *"silence, PLEASE."* She has to call Alice's name twice, and Alice squeaks and knocks her messenger bag off the desk before getting up.

I almost smile, but the sight of everyone standing up and looking everywhere but at me stops me. I let my hair hang down in my face and stare at the floor. Then I lean over and stare more closely.

"Alice, are those ... Why do you have giant metallic Sharpies?" I ask slowly.

The pens rolling around are the huge Super Sharpies, each as thick as three normal markers, in colors like metallic blue, orange, bronze, and so on. The kind that were used to draw all over my work.

I look up. "Alice?" I say again, and I can't help it, my voice cracks a little.

Everyone freezes. Alice looks at me, then lifts her chin. "What?" she says, her voice belligerent. "They're pens. I like to draw. I—"

"Where did you get them?" I ask.

Alice looks down. "I don't ... I don't know. I don't remember. I've had them a while." She bends down and starts shoving them in a bag, and I stare at the creepy thing sticking out of her head, wondering how well I know anybody.

CHAPTER 25

And the Worst Part Is That I Can't Even Feel Sorry for Myself Anymore, but at Least I Drove Away My Last Ally

Alice.

Alice?

Alice, who wants to make friends, and who does sick special effects, and who brought in a cookie for Molly? Alice, who has a giant bronze Sharpie in her bag and doesn't seem to want to talk about it? The world tips a little bit, and I stare. The vertigo feeling comes back, and I desperately wish I were anywhere else. I open my mouth, then close it, because what is there to say, really?

Alice doesn't look at me.

Before I can think of something, Ms. Lewiston walks in.

Ms. Davis gives another theatrical glance at her watch, then at Ms. Lewiston. "Ah. Finally. Can you please ensure that the room is put back the way it needs to be for class next week, then escort the students under suspicion to my office?" Without waiting for a reply, she says, "Thank you," and stomps out of the room.

Ms. Lewiston looks tired.

"Jax's father is picking him up to get his head checked, though he didn't black out, and there doesn't seem to be a risk of concussion." She drops into the chair next to me and turns, a half smile on her face. "Silver lining, I guess?"

Silver lining. That's another of my dad's favorite sayings. Or at least, it used to be. . . . Who knows if he still says it anymore. Any catastrophe, any dropped eggs or missed flights or spilled milk, he'd find something totally irrelevant to remark on, then smile and say, "Hashtag silver lining, right?" Hearing Ms. Lewiston say it doesn't help my mood. At all. I don't smile back, and her face falls.

"Look, Theo. I understand how you must—" she starts, but I shake my head. Hard.

Oh good. That anger I wanted earlier is showing up. It floods through me, and suddenly I'm too mad to even look at Lewiston's face. I don't want to see her worry or sadness. This whole freaking disaster is her fault, and I cannot— I WILL not—listen to any more of her garbage.

"STOP. Just . . . stop." My voice is louder than I meant it to be.

"Theo," she starts again, but I stand up, kicking my chair back so that it crashes into the one behind it.

"NO! You don't get to tell me it's all part of the process. That everyone's fighting a battle and all that crap. I don't care. I don't want to hear it. I don't want to feel sorry for Molly and her stupid falling-apart family. Or freak-show Alice, who by the way, is carrying around a bunch of giant Sharpies like the ones that ruined my work! Did you know that? Yeah. I don't know what the story is with any of you losers. We've been here all week, and you know what I learned? NOTHING. Someone hates me. Someone thinks it's a real joke to ruin the art I made. To—again and again—destroy MY ART. And maybe they had a troubled childhood or a traumatic summer but I. Don't. Care." I pick up the stupid fake candle, which Alice put on the windowsill, and fling it toward the front of the room. It bounces once and rolls away, not even giving me the satisfaction of breaking.

Ms. Lewiston looks even sadder. "But you do care, Theo, and that's a good thing. I know you don't want to hear it, but everyone is fighting—"

"An unseen battle. Yeah, whatever. You're wrong. I don't care about them, or about your ramalama-ding-dong Justice Circle, which just wasted a lot of time and made us all play nice for a few hours before everyone went back to their corners and I'm left exactly where I started! My stuff is ruined! But you know what?" I walk away from her, because I'm so mad I can't stand still, can't look at her stupid worried face another second.

I stare out the window. "The worst thing isn't even that my photos were trashed. The worst part"—my voice cracks and I want to punch something, want to take a hammer to the whole display of dioramas and poster boards on the windowsill—"the worst part is that one of these losers hates me enough to do it. Again and again. And that, thanks to you and your STUPID idea, I get to think that whoever did it might actually be a decent person. So knowing they hate me feels even worse." I shut my mouth, hard. Big ugly snot-filled sobs want out, but there is no way I'm crying here.

"Oh, Theo," Ms. Lewiston starts, but I shake my head.

Erik comes toward me, his big meathead face concerned. "Hey, buddy—"

But I put up my hands. "Stop talking. STOP TALKING! Seriously, you're *one* sports metaphor away from being a crappy Nike ad. God, you're an idiot! No one cares what you have to say except your stupid friends, and you guys deserve each other."

Erik steps back, his face as red as if I slapped him. But I don't care. At all.

I look around. "All of you! You think you're such special snowflakes, with your own unique stories. But you're just boring and average and sad. And honestly, shame on me, because for a hot minute, I thought you were something more too, but you're not! You're exactly what you seem: an Overachiever, a Jock, a Weirdo, a Nerd, and a Screwup." I shake my head. "Just. Go. Away."

Alice moves first, quietly picking up her bag and heading for the door. One by one the others follow her out.

Ms. Lewiston walks toward me, but whatever she sees in my face stops her from coming closer. We stare at each other for a second, and I turn back to the window.

"I'll give you some space," she says.

The last shreds of my rage flare up. "Give me ALL my space!" I shout. "Davis is right. You made it worse. This whole thing was your fault! From now on leave me alone!"

It feels good to say it, like I fed the beast that was so, so hungry. Ms. Lewiston puts her hands over her stomach, like she got punched. But she nods and tries to smile, and all the good anger drains out of me so fast I'm dizzy.

"I'm sorry, Theo," she says quietly, walking to the door. "For everything."

I'm left by myself.

* * *

I cry for a while. Big loud noisy hiccupy sobs that I don't even try to hide. They don't last long. After my dad left, I learned to cry as fast as possible, getting out the bare minimum so I could look normal before my mom saw me. By the time she asked, I always said I was fine. That was when she started me on allergy medicine, because my nose and eyes were always red. But my voice sounded normal, and she didn't have to keep dropping to her knees to hug me and hold me and try to keep her own tears in, so it worked, I guess. Even now it's probably barely two minutes before I'm wiping my nose on my sleeve and looking around.

Anyway, no one hears, because there's no one around. Our group, if we were ever a group, is scattered—Jax to the doctor, the others to "real" detention, and now Ms. Lewiston to wherever teachers go when everything goes wrong. Her face—frozen and trying to smile—flashes in my mind, and I curl up in the chair. What will happen now? Will she get fired? Will she ignore me in the halls on Monday? Am I supposed to apologize?

A flare of anger starts back up. This *was* all her fault, though. I was fine being a loner in this school. I was fine not hanging my art on the walls where people could see it and make fun of me. I was fine not feeling sorry for Molly or laughing with Alice or thinking Erik was actually a pretty decent guy or cracking up with Jax. I. Was. Fine.

And now? Now, thanks to Ms. Lewiston, I'm not fine. I was lying, just like they lied to me. Because after this week, despite what I said, I know they're not just the Overachiever, the Jock, the Weirdo, the Nerd, and the Screwup. They're actually fairly cool. They're good people. Except that someone, or maybe everyone, is lying. Someone destroyed my art again and again, and lied about it. And if sort of cool people do that to my photos, what does that make me? I'm not fine at all.

I don't say anything to my mom in the car, and when we get home, I go straight to my room. I flop facedown on my bed, smushed into my pillow. I don't know if I'm there fifteen minutes or an hour before there's a quiet knock on the door.

"Theo, love? You okay in there?"

I grunt.

"Can I come in?"

I'm tempted to say no, to tell her to leave me alone, and I know if I do she will, at least for a while. She's good like that, mostly, once she's convinced herself I'm not in here trying to build a bomb or something. But I give an affirmative grunt, and the door opens.

"Hey," she says, carefully crossing my skateboard-and-laundry-strewn room. "How did things go today? You okay?"

I shrug, still facedown. Part of me wants to tell her what happened, but another part doesn't want her worry and pity and sadness to sit on top of my own. Mine is bad enough.

She sits on the edge of my bed and rubs my back. "Sweet son . . . ," she starts.

But I sit up fast and move away, to the back wall. "Don't," I say. "Just . . . don't." I wrap my arms around my knees and let my hair fall down.

"Was it really bad?" she asks, her voice almost a whisper.

I shake my head, then shrug. "Yeah." That's the only word I get out before a sob tears out of me, so deep and hard I feel like I'm ripping in two.

I snortsobcrysnortsob all over my knees, soaking my jeans with tears and snot. I don't know how long I cry, but when I pause, I realize my mom has both arms around me, holding me tight.

I look up, trying to catch my breath. "It's just . . ." I hiccup another sob. "WHY? Why do they hate me? Am I that bad?" I bury my face again and wish I could disappear, that I could curl up into something so small that it could get lost, rolled down a gutter or vacuumed up without anyone even noticing.

"Oh, *Theo*," my mom says, and her voice is so sad that I cry harder.

I don't say what's pulsing through my brain:

I have no friends.

My dad doesn't even stay in touch.

Kids at school go out of their way to torture me, to laugh at me, to make the most *me* part of myself, my photos, the ground zero for humiliation and pain.

I'm alone and so lonely no one even likes me.

I'm about as pathetic as a person can be.

I don't say any of this. I sob and sob until I don't have anything left.

After, my mom tries to get me to get up, shower, and go get dinner. She offers Thai food as an enticement, but I'm not interested. Finally, after trying a few times, she pulls up the blankets and tucks me in. When she turns out the light, I realize how tired I am—how deep-down-to-my-bones tired. I have no idea what time it is, but I fall asleep.

CHAPTER 26

How Does It Feel to Get a Lesson in Truth from a Five-Year-Old? Let Me Tell You All About It.

I sleep like a dead person and wake up with a headache that feels like my brain is fighting its way out of my skull. Also, my stomach is all kinds of messed up. I need the bathroom. Fast. When I finally zombie walk to the breakfast table, my mom looks worried.

"How are you?" she asks. "You feeling okay?" She knows all too well that when I get nervous, it mostly shows in the appalling smells that come out of the bathroom.

"Totally fine. Must have eaten a bad clam," I answer, avoiding her eye.

This is an ongoing joke between us, from a vacation when I was ten when my dad spent the whole five days vomiting spectacularly loudly in our tiny hotel bathroom. He was convinced it was "just a bad clam," though my mom eventually had the local doctor shoot him full of penicillin for the massive bacterial infection he was fighting.

She side-eyes me, then slides over a bowl of oatmeal. "Yeah, I don't think so. Theo, about last night—"

"Mom, I'm fine. Sorry I was so emo and angsty. I mean, I was legit upset, but that was over-the-top. I'm fine." I look right at her, trying to convince her, despite what she saw and heard, that I'm not a quivering mess.

She shakes her head. "I'm glad you feel better, but we're going to talk about it. Theo, you have to understand, just because something happened to your photos doesn't mean people don't like you."

I look up, and the expression on my face makes her back up.

"Okay! Okay, it seems like *someone* doesn't like you, but that's one person! Not everyone! Theo, you are a very aloof kid! There are times I'm intimidated to talk to you, and I'm your mom!"

I ignore her and keep spooning honey into my oatmeal.

"Look." She falls silent.

She's quiet so long I look up and wind up dripping honey all over the table. "What," I finally say, in a voice that's as uninviting as possible.

"I think you should go in today. NO! Hear me out," she

says as I open my mouth to tell her all the reasons that's a spectacularly bad idea. "Listen. You made real progress with that Justice Circle, and Ms. Lewiston has given a lot of time to the process. You agreed to go even though you didn't have to— Hear me out!" she says again, because I'm not having any of this. "You did, Theo. You agreed to do it, and I think you should go down there and finish the job."

I nod slowly, then say, "No. Nope, no way, but thanks anyway. I did my part. I did everything I could, okay?"

"Did you?"

They are just two little words, but they stop me.

Did I do everything I could?

Well, no. Not really. I didn't actually want to know. I didn't tell Erik I saw his phone. I didn't push Alice for answers. I went along with it, but honestly, I never really wanted this Justice Circle to work, because if it worked, I'd have to stare right at whoever did it.

But still. I did enough. I did all I'm going to do.

"Well?" she asks. "I feel strongly about this. I can drop you off this morning, and you can know that no matter what happens today, you stuck with it."

I look down at my food, and my mom reaches over and lifts my chin, brushing my hair out of my face.

"It is that bad?" she whispers.

I swallow hard and move away. I don't want to be Theo-the-pathetic, Theo-the-weak, Theo-the-pitied.

"Fine," I say, shaking my hair back down. "Fine, I'll go." What I don't say is that I'll go hang out in room 201 and read until it's time for pickup. Because while I don't want to fight with my mom on top of everything else, I know, with total certainty, that this is over.

"Really? You'll do it? Do you think you might be willing to talk a bit more with people there, and maybe share more with them?" She sounds ridiculously pleased, which makes me equal parts glad I lied and deeply ashamed of it.

"Yeah, well, I'll think about showing . . . erm, I mean sharing, more of my . . . More. Self. Stuff." I say this through a huge bit of oatmeal, which I think helps the situation.

My mom looks like she's trying incredibly hard not to pry my mouth open, Hulk-style, and make me talk actual words that make sense. But I guess she's learned something in twenty years of being a librarian, because she nods like I said something reasonable, and not something that sounds like it came out of Google Translate's Ukrainian-to-English app.

"Well, I know you know this, but I'll tell you again. I'm really proud of you. It would have been easy to refuse to engage, but you didn't. You're my brave son."

She kisses me on top of my head, then wrinkles her

nose. "Did you manage to get honey *in* your hair? How? Seriously, how do you do that?"

I shrug and she laughs and points to the shower. "Make it fast. I can't be late."

As I planned, when my mom drops me off, I avoid the office and head right to room 201. It smells weird now that it's empty. The clock ticks in a bizarre insect-buzz way, and the radiator makes a faint clicking noise every few seconds. It was never this quiet in here, even when we were supposed to be working. Someone was always shifting or scratching or whispering or tapping their feet or something. Now it's just me, and I don't move.

In theory I can get comfortable and read the stack of graphic novels I brought. But even though I wanted to be alone, it feels all wrong. There's no reason to be here anymore. No Justice Circle. No Ms. Lewiston coming back with Starbursts. No wondering what special effects Alice will have next.

Nope, the SS *Theo Has Friends* has sailed away, and all that's left are the inevitable awkward moments when we see each other next week. Once they're back from suspension, of course. Because they'll be super excited to see me at that point. Maybe someone will confess today. Who knows? Maybe Davis has a whole system of breaking down tweenbot semi-criminals and will have an answer by noon. But I won't be in the room to find out.

From outside the door I hear footsteps and a deep whistling tune. The whistling stops, and Mr. Saunders, the janitor, laughs, sounding way too happy.

"I told you, you only have to be here an hour this morning, then Mama's coming to pick you up. All you got to do is take out the garbage and you'll be done twice as quick!" he says.

A high giggle answers, and the door swings open. Mr. Saunders rolls in the giant trash can, and behind him runs a kid who can't be more than four or five.

"Daddyyyy!" he calls. "I told you! I can't reach." He races to the big garbage and tries to throw in a candy wrapper, but he's way shorter than the bin, and the wrapper floats to the ground.

Mr. Saunders laughs again and picks it up. "That's okay, Li'l Bit. I'll go extra fast, and we'll be done soon. And then . . ."

"Then Mama's taking me to the MOVIES! And popcorn!" he shouts.

Mr. Saunders catches sight of me and stops short. "Oh, hey there, my man. Sorry to interrupt. I'm doing the easy stuff first today, as I have a VIP with me. This is my son Teddy John."

Teddy John looks over at me, his eyes wide. I wonder if I look like some kind of blotchy, angsty middle school demon, but he smiles big. He's missing a front tooth, like he's a poster for cute.

"Yeah, his mom had to run into work this morning, so Teddy's hanging with me for a little while, on the down low," Mr. Saunders continues. "You were a big help the other day, when Mama had to work, and today we're moving even faster, isn't that right?" He winks at his son.

"Sorry," I say, standing up and pulling my bag onto the seat. "I can move."

Mr. Saunders waves me down. "You're good," he says. "We'll only be a minute."

He starts emptying the classroom garbage cans into the big container, while Teddy John jumps around, singing something about a bat and a cat. I think. Anyway, I'm about to start reading again when he calls, "Daddy! I found more trash!"

Mr. Saunders and I both turn to find him holding the little electric candle, which rolled under a desk after I threw it.

I stare at the candle, then at the boy, who's now running it toward the trash and trying to fling it up over the side.

"Hey." My voice sounds like I'm gargling gravel, so I cough and try again.

"Mr. Saunders? Did you— Um. The other day, when

you cleaned this room, did you find some . . ." Well. What would they look like, if you had no idea? ". . . some boxes on the floor? One was tin, one was plastic, and another one—"

Teddy John nods, his head moving so fast his face blurs. "I sure did. I found them and I threw them out because I'm helping!"

Mr. Saunders pauses. "What's all this?" he asks. "What boxes? Li'l Bit, did you throw something away that wasn't trash?"

"Nope! It was trash. It was on the floor. And the desk." He looks up at me, all big brown eyes and missing tooth. "Right?"

"Actually . . ." I sit back down and scrub my face with my hand. I'm So. Freaking. Tired. I open my eyes. Teddy John is still watching me, now biting his lip. His eyebrows are all scrunched up, and he reminds me of Molly.

I try to smile, though I'm pretty sure it looks like I've been punched somewhere sensitive. "It actually, um. It wasn't trash. Believe it or not, those were cameras. Pinhole cameras, they're called, and I made them myself. But they don't look like anything special, I guess. They were . . . I can see that you'd think they were garbage. I mean, if you didn't know."

Mr. Saunders straightens up from where he was wiping down the chairs and comes over. He peers down at me. "So let me get this right. Did we throw out something important?"

His son starts to talk, but he puts a big hand on his shoulder. "Hush up for a minute, TJ, and let the boy talk."

"But I didn't . . . ," he starts to say; then he sees his father's expression and stays quiet.

I look at his face, which is now pinched and worried. The last thing I want to do is make him feel bad. Making a five-year-old sob would be quite the grand finale for the epic of misery that I've spread far and wide. I sigh.

"Um. Well, yeah. They weren't *that* important, but I didn't know what happened to them. And I—I mean, all of us—we came in and they were gone, or messed up, and we assumed . . . I mean, we figured someone had done it on purpose."

Mr. Saunders shakes his head real slow. "Well, that's too darn bad. And I'm sorry." He looks down at Teddy John. "What do you say, Li'l Bit? I know you didn't do it on purpose, and you were helping me out, but it sounds like maybe we threw out something that this boy . . . you're Theo, right? Theo with the photographs? Anyway, we might have made a mistake and thrown out something Theo cared about."

Teddy John gazes up at me. "I'm sorry, Theo," he says. He straightens his back and puts his hands on his hips, like he's going to launch into a song.

I blink and step back.

"I 'pologize! I didn't mean to, but my teacher always says 'actions matter' and my action was to throw out your boxes and I'm so sorry and I can help you make a new one or give you my allowance to buy one or—"

I raise my hand, but he just keeps talking.

"Or I can hug you if you're feeling sad, because I am taking 'sponsibility for my actions," he finishes proudly.

Mr. Saunders gives him a squeeze. "That's a nice way to apologize," he says.

And I nod. Because seriously, that was like an elite-level professional apology. "It's cool," I say, and I squat down at eye level. "They weren't *that* big a deal. I'm just really glad to know what happened to them." I hold my hand out, and Teddy John slaps me a high five, hard. Kid's got serious guns. . . . Erik should start training him up.

"It's cool," he echoes, and then pulls his dad's hand. "Are we almost done? Because MOVIE!! And POPCORN!"

When they leave, I stay standing in the middle of the room like someone planted me there.

Seriously? Mr. Saunders's kid accidentally threw them out?

I think about Ms. Lewiston's statement the first day, that intentions and actions are not always the same thing, and that people are fighting battles we can't see. I'm sure

Mr. Saunders didn't mess up my work the first two times, but he sure proved that I don't always have a clue what's going on.

I try to sit down and keep reading, but my mind keeps wandering. Teddy John Saunders. My cameras. Jax's yoga-ball soccer. Molly's hands trembling. Alice smiling with a severed finger stuck behind her ear.

Everyone's fighting an unseen battle.

I close the book.

Before I can think too hard about it, I take off running down the hall toward Davis's office.

I want to be with them. I want to know what happened. I want to know the truth. Ms. Lewiston will be there, and we can try to actually do this Justice Circle thing. Though with Ms. Davis right there . . . The very thought of trying to talk with her there makes me want to lie down in traffic. As fast as I start running, I stop.

I pause and run back toward Mr. Saunders. He's coming out of room 205, whistling away. Teddy John's bouncing ahead of him.

"Hey, Mr. Saunders," I start, and I don't even know what I'm going to tell him until the words come spilling out. I explain, as quickly as possible, what went down: my stuff being ruined, Ms. Lewiston wanting to do this Justice Circle, Ms. Davis saying it's no use, and the rest of it.

"But here's the thing," I say. "I really think there's a chance that we were getting somewhere. And you know, these last cameras . . . it wasn't bullying or vandalism or anything, it was—"

"Teddy," he finishes. "So." He fixes me with a stare. "What exactly are you asking?"

I gulp. Fortune favors the bold, as Alice likes to tell us. Usually with a fake scalpel embedded in her forearm. I decide to go for it. "Do you think it's possible you could be in need of Principal Davis's time today? For, um . . . as much of the day as possible?"

Mr. Saunders sighs so big I can smell his mint gum and feel the gust move my hair.

"I'm sorry," I say, and my cheeks are burning. I shake my hair until it's mostly in front of my face. "I know you're busy. That was a stupid thing to ask. Never—"

Mr. Saunders shakes his head, but he starts to smile, then lets out a short laugh. "That's okay. Kids ask me to do all kinds of things around here, and I mean *alllllll* kinds of things. They lose their phones and beg me to find 'em before their parents find out. Or don't study for a test and ask if I can pull the fire alarm for a fire drill. Or tell me they forgot a roast beef sandwich in their locker and can I come clean it out because it smells nasty." He sighs.

"You're a good kid, Theo. You didn't deserve what

happened to your photographs. They were beautiful, and brave."

My cheeks burn at the compliment, and I try to say thank you, but it comes out as a bleat. Awesome.

He goes on. "And Kate Lewiston is a good teacher." He pauses, then speaks again. "Ms. Davis is a mighty organized person, and she likes to keep a tight rein on every aspect of the school. I've been meaning to ask her to give an opinion on our supply closet and our product suppliers. Think we might be able to save some serious money if we were to reorganize and then place larger-size orders. Might be a good day to get her eyes on that project. Seeing as it's a quiet week and all. Give me two minutes and I'll see what I can do."

I exhale and smile, a big stupid chipmunk-face smile. "Thank you. Seriously. Thanks. I mean it. Thank—"

He waves me off. "World's hard enough, man. We all got to do what we can. Am I right?" Clapping me on the shoulder, Mr. Saunders turns and starts walking away, to where Teddy John's waiting down the hall.

"Right," I say to his retreating back. "Right." I wait two minutes, then sprint down the hall toward Davis's office.

CHAPTER 27

Once More into the Breach I Go, This Time with a Plan. (Sort of. Ish.)

When I get outside the office, I stop. While it seemed noble to burst in there and demand the truth, I'm now seriously doubting the wisdom of this plan. The hot rush of humiliation is still like a virus, eating away at my guts, and I really don't want to talk about it. I tried to do the justice thing, and it didn't work. I still have the choice to just . . . *not*. Even worse, the ugly words I shouted yesterday repeat in my head like a bad Justin Bieber song, and I wish more than anything I'd never said them. They were downright cruel, and the memory of everyone's faces makes me cringe. A gross honest part of me knows that if I'd stayed quiet, I could at least still feel like the victim. Now my words feel like a weapon I've thrown right back.

But I keep picturing my mom asking me if I did everything I could, and I gird my loins (or at least clench my butt cheeks) and throw open the door.

I walk toward the small conference room off the main office, and even before I get there, I know that my hapless fellow Justice Circle inmates are there. The door's half open, and I peer through before opening it the rest of the way. Jax is jiggling both legs while pushing back on the chair so it rests on the rear legs. It looks precarious, and given the white bandage on his head from yesterday's drama, I can't help thinking it's a bad idea. Next to him Andre is staring at the conference table, his hands moving fast but silently on top of it. Drumming, I guess. I try to imagine loud death metal sounds coming from him, but my mind refuses to make the leap. Alice, next to Andre, is disappointingly tame today. There's a small gash above her eyebrow, but that's it. Clearly, she's phoning it in. And Molly and Erik are on either side of Ms. Lewiston, their backs to me, their heads down.

The room is silent.

I want to say something funny, or clever, at least, but nothing comes to mind, except, once again, Ms. Lewiston's note on that first day. "Be kind . . ."

Instead of saying something awesome, I fake cough so pathetically that I immediately wish for a "delete" button so I can do it over. Tragically, I attempt to make it better by doing an even *worse* fake cough, like it was a joke the whole time.

"HEM HEM HEM," I say, in a sad, Dolores Umbridge sort of way. Maybe they'll think I'm being ironic.

Alice jumps up. "Theo!" she calls, her voice as bright and singsongy as ever. "Did you come to yell at us some more?"

I say something that sounds like *glargeblarglemimbles-turtp*.

Awesome.

Jax lets his chair fall with a *thunk*. "Seriously? You came back? You're the only one who had a free pass out of here. Trust me, this is *not* where you want to be. Is this some kind of sympathy move? If so, you're making a heck of a sacrifice. Because Davis was on *fire* this morning. Though she left a minute ago, which felt like a gift from the gods. Sorry, Ms. Lewiston."

Ms. Lewiston has turned around in her chair to stare at me, and she waves a hand absently at Jax.

He goes on. "Also, you pack any provisions, if you know what I mean?" He waggles his eyebrows and mouths *"Angel tears!"*

I swallow and try again. "Nah. I mean, I came to tell you guys something. And to ask you something." I glance at Ms. Lewiston, whose expression is hard to read. "And also to, you know. Apologize. Because I said some stuff yesterday that I shouldn't have said, and it wasn't even true, so that makes it even stupider. So . . . sorry." I look at Ms. Lewiston. "I'm really sorry."

Ms. Lewiston stands up and is over to me in three steps. The woman is around six feet tall, and today she's wearing big stomping boots that make her look like an Amazon. Ms. Davis better watch out.

"Theo, you don't need to apologize to me," she says. "You've been a . . . well, you've been a really good participant in this process, no matter what." She looks around. "I have to say, you are all such good kids. I don't know . . ." Her voice trails off. "Well, anyway. What did you want to tell us, Theo?"

"Here, man. Have a seat over here. I'll move," Erik says, springing to his feet. He's wearing jeans and a flannel shirt instead of polyester sports pants and a hoodie, and as he moves by me, I get a whiff of some nasty Axe body spray. I try not to wince. He's clearly pulling out the big guns for Alice. I hope for his sake she's able to overlook the scent overload.

"I just want to say," Molly says, before I can speak, "we were all pretty upset yesterday, and, Theo, whatever, I understand that you're mad. But what I *don't* get is that we wanted to talk about what had happened, but Ms. Davis made us sit in silence! Like, actual silence." She glares around. "I mean, I thought we were supposed to, you know, *process* it and stuff."

Ms. Lewiston sighs. "I'm sorry, Molly. I should have come in to facilitate. I'm really sorry I wasn't there for you."

She doesn't make excuses or say that the reason she bailed was that I was a total jerk to her and she needed to be alone. I remember Teddy John's apology, his "taking responsibility for his actions," and decide to speak up.

"I'm sorry too. Part of that was my fault."

Jax, who had leaned back again, slams his chair down. "Dude, what do you keep apologizing for? That's messed up. It's your stuff that got ruined. I mean, someone is straight up playing us, and—"

I cut him off. "No, wait! That's part of why I wanted to come in. I was alone in room 201 this morning, and Mr. Saunders and his little boy came in. He's, like, five years old or something, but he's coming to work with him this week, because his mom's got extra shifts. Anyway, he was helping Mr. Saunders clean." As quickly as I can, I explain what happened: how he found the candle, then I asked about the cameras, then he told me he had thrown them out, not realizing.

"And then he apologized, and, I mean, Ms. Lewiston, if you had heard him, you'd have promoted him to the head of the Justice Circle or whatever. He literally offered to help make new ones or give me his allowance or just hug me because he was 'taking responsibility for his actions.' It was like . . ." I clear my throat, which has gotten a little stupid-scratchy. "Well, it was pretty cool."

I stare down at my hands, because all six of the other people in the room are staring at me, and I'm going kind of walleyed trying to make eye contact with them all. But then I look up.

"So here's the thing. Ms. Lewiston, you told us the first day that intentions aren't always the same as actions, and now I find out that Mr. Saunders's cute little five-year-old who doesn't even know me destroyed my cameras, and it's totally fine. I mean, it's too bad about the shots, but honestly, it's such a huge freaking relief that it wasn't any of you."

I look at each of them in turn. Molly is pink and a little shocked, Alice has her head cocked to one side like a bird or something, Andre's shaking his head a little, and Erik looks like he might cry. Even Jax is totally still, his whole body tucked tight in the chair.

"Because . . ." I pause and look at Ms. Lewiston. "I actually thought this week was pretty good. It wasn't how I wanted to spend my vacation, but I mean, watching Molly freak out over Starbursts"—I grin at her, and to my relief she grins back—"that alone was worth it. Not to mention Alice! No offense to the rest of you, but, Alice, your special effects stuff was literally the highlight of each day. I would start wondering what you'd have going on before I even left my house in the morning."

Alice gives a pleased-sounding squeak and wriggles a little. *"Thank* you," she says, beaming. "If you ever want to star as a tortured artist turned zombie, I could *totally* work with your hair-and-hat combo. Scene could start with you looking through a big camera, so the lens obscures most of your face, but when you lower it, we see you've got strips of flesh peeling down . . ."

I cough. "Wow." I glance at Andre, who shrugs, like *Bro, you asked for it, you deal with it.* Thanks for nothing.

"Anyway, and hearing about Skeleton Curse, and playing yoga-ball soccer in the gym—" I look at Erik, who reaches across to high-five me, then at Ms. Lewiston. "Um. Pretend you didn't hear that."

"Hear what?" Ms. Lewiston asks. She has her head down and is rummaging in her bag. "I didn't hear anything. So sorry."

I nod. "Yeah. Anyway, I guess all I'm saying is that it was a surprisingly okay week, and I actually assumed I knew everything I needed to know about you guys after seven years of school together. But it turns out I don't know much. And definitely not the important stuff." I think about Molly's brother, and her Lady of Shalott face, and her signing all her permission slips and report cards. "And I should have never said what I said yesterday. Because I don't even think it's true. Not anymore.

"And you guys remember what Ms. Lewiston wrote on the board that first day? 'Be kind, for all of us are fighting unseen battles'? Well, I guess I'm saying I don't think any of you would trash my work on purpose. I just don't believe it." I look at Erik. "And I want you to tell me the truth, no matter what."

I go silent and look down at the table again. My heart is suddenly pounding, and my pits are sweaty. For the first time the fluorescent lighting and big round table seem like a terrible place for any kind of brave and honest confession. I want dark corners and noise and a place to hide. But there's nothing but six faces and a silent room.

CHAPTER 28

The Truth, the Whole Truth, and Nothing but the Truth? Maybe.

I don't know what to say next or where to look. Dimly, in the back of my mind, I realize that this might be the dumbest thing I've ever done, dumber even than putting those photos up in the first place. Because there was no reason—no reason at all—for me to walk into this room. The drumbeat starts in my head.

Stupid.

Stupid.

Stupid.

Then Molly speaks. "'Speak the truth, even if your voice shakes.'" She swallows. "I read that somewhere. I . . . um." She falls silent.

My heart, if anything, speeds up. Molly? Molly with the dead brother? Molly, whose past year has made my poor-little-Theo-his-parents-got-divorced life seem like a picnic? Seriously?

She looks at me, then down at the table, so that all I can see is the top of her head, her braids so tight I can see her scalp.

"On Tuesday I stayed late for student council, and my mom forgot. . . . I didn't have a ride home. So I had to wait until six-thirty, when my dad got home. And after doing my homework in the computer lab I went to the student gallery, to wait. And a bunch of guys . . . Kevin, Jude, Blaine— you know?" She looks at me.

I nod. Of course I know Blaine Travis. He's . . . well, I'd say he's a cliché of a total bully, like Biff from that old movie *Back to the Future*. But maybe after this week I have to wonder. Maybe he's got some kind of horrible stuff going on in his life too. I sigh. It was a lot easier when I could be Judgy McJudgeface.

"Yeah, I know Blaine. He and Kevin Hellson"—of the giant zit—"spent fourth grade telling everyone I was gay. Not that there's anything wrong with it if I *was*. But—"

Molly nods. "Yeah. He called my brother a retard when they did baseball together one summer. Which was really not cool, since my brother actually *was* developmentally delayed." She swallows so loudly we can all hear it, then goes on. "Anyway, Jude, Blaine, Kevin, and Shaun Wender were in there, cracking up, jumping around, and . . ." Her voice trails off. "And trashing your photos. And I walked right in, not even paying attention at first—" Molly starts to cry but keeps talking, and my own face is hot in sympathy.

". . . and they dared me to do it, to take a marker and draw something, and I didn't . . . I just . . ." Her sobs become so loud it's hard to understand her, and I stare.

Ms. Lewiston stands up and puts her hand on Molly's shoulder. But Molly shakes her off. When she starts talking again, her voice is like broken glass, loud and jagged and sharp. "Everything's wrong! EVERYTHING. I'm failing math and Spanish. And my mom . . . my mom just sleeps and cries. Nothing is okay anymore! And they were in my face, like it was all a big joke. And . . . I . . . I just wanted to destroy something! I wanted to make something else be as ruined and awful and ugly as everything in my life, and just for that one second, for that one second when I held that gold Sharpie, I didn't care. About anything! And it was such a relief. And I drew one line, one big, horrible zigzag, and I felt so awful, Theo. I swear, I would do anything—ANYTHING—to take it back."

She sobs, and no one speaks. Finally she looks up. Her eyes are red and swollen, and she looks ruined.

"I'm sorry, Theo. I'm so, so sorry."

I open my mouth and close it again. I want to say something, tell her it's okay, but what comes out in a weird frog voice is "What happened next?"

She swallows, hard. "They heard footsteps and ran. They all went flying out the side door, and I just . . . I just stood there. Then a second later Jax and Erik came in the other door, and Alice came in, and, and . . . and . . ."

"And you yelled for Davis," I finished. I shook my head.

Molly Claremont.

Molly, the Overachiever.

Molly, the sister of a dead boy.

Molly, who wanted, just for a second, to destroy something.

My mind flies back to the week after my dad told me he was leaving, how I went into my room and methodically smashed all my old Lego models—the fancy hundred-dollar sets that had taken months to build—smashed them to nothing. How deeply *good* it felt, then how bad.

I nod slowly. "Yeah. I get it," I say.

Molly stares at me, and her face looks a million years old. "I'm so sorry. I'm just. So sorry." She puts her head down on her folded arms and sobs.

"Breathe, Molly," Ms. Lewiston says softly. "Lean back and breathe. Slow, deep breaths."

Like robots, all six of us fall back in our chairs. I try

taking one of those yoga breaths, like my mom does, and—go figure—my body relaxes.

Slowly Molly's sobs quiet. "I should have told," she says, her voice flat. "Even after. I should have told."

"Why didn't you?" Alice asks, her voice quieter than usual. "Tell, I mean."

Molly wraps her arms around herself and shakes her head. Her tears have stopped, but I can tell from her red face and bunched-up eyebrows that she's a hot minute from losing it.

"I don't know," she whispers. "I'm just so tired. I'm so freaking tired. And I knew they'd say I had done it too, and they'd be right." She looks up at me, and her face isn't frozen or cursed, it's just so sad. "I'm sorry, Theo. I should have said something. It was a terrible thing to do."

In the silence, Alice speaks up. "I did the same thing, I think."

We all look at her. My stomach, which had calmed slightly with my yoga breathing, clenches again. "What do you mean? Were you there too?" I ask. The sweaty feeling comes back. Was everyone in on it?

But Alice shakes her head, her dark eyes solemn. "No, I wasn't there. But when Blaine and Kevin and Shaun and Jude came running out, they nearly ran right into me. And they . . ." Her voice is low. "They threw the Sharpies at me. Hard. One of them actually drew blood." She pulls back her bangs, and we can see the remains of an angry red welt on her forehead. "Anyway, they called me a bunch of names, which they always do, and said the markers were a gift. A gift for the freak. Then they kicked my bag down the hall and ran away."

She pauses, and a wave of . . . I don't know, sadness, or something . . . crashes over me. It must be exhaustingly, endlessly hard to be Alice.

"Anyway, I bent down to pick up my stuff, and the Sharpies they threw, and then I heard Molly yelling. When I went in, I knew right away who had done it. But I didn't want to tell. I didn't want them to— Well. To be meaner than they already are." She looks at me. "But that wasn't fair. And I'm sorry. I should have said something."

Andre coughs. "I would have done the same thing. Heck, I *have* done the same thing, though in my case I actually saw it. I saw Kevin messing with Ms. Bellante's sheet music and instruments before music class once, and I pretended I hadn't seen anything. I didn't want beef with him. It's hard enough keeping out of stuff. . . . There was no way I was going to get into that. And that was the day Ms. Bellante cried in class, remember? And we all got that big lecture?"

We all nod. Hapless Ms. Bellante is an easy target, because (1) she's really young; (2) she's way too earnest about music for the grunts of Shipton Middle School; and (3) she has class after recess Friday afternoons. Talk about prey . . . she's like a fluffy-eared bunny in a pack of wolves.

"Anyway, I get it," Andre says.

I close my eyes. My brain plays a video for me, reminding me that my until-recently super-successful technique of staying out of people's business meant walking right by locker fights, reading a book when some poor nerd got pelted with food in the cafeteria, talking to Mateo or double-knotting my laces when I heard crap going down in PE.

Opening my eyes, I look at Molly, then at Alice and Andre. "Truth? I would have done the exact same thing," I say finally.

Molly sniffs a little and nods. "Still," she says.

"Yeah," I say. "Still. Thanks for telling me."

Erik coughs.

I look over. Erik Estrale, my number one suspect, jock extraordinaire, and teammate of at least two of the guys who did this. I think about those texts on his phone again.

"I need . . . I want to say something." He looks at Ms. Lewiston, and she nods slightly.

"You guys probably think that since Kevin and those

guys are on the team, I knew all about this, or maybe that I did it," he starts.

I look down.

"Well, I didn't. I had no idea. Or at least, I didn't until a few days ago, when they started bragging about it in the locker room. This was the first day I made it to basketball camp—the first time I'd seen them all week. At first I didn't know what they were talking about, and I didn't really care. I was so pumped to be back with the team. And they're always fronting about something. . . . I kind of tune it out, you know? I mean, they're my friends. Or . . . they were." He pauses. "But then I figured out what they were talking about, and I straight up asked them." He flushes bright red and presses his lips together. "And they said . . . well, it doesn't matter. But it wasn't cool. It wasn't cool at all. And I told them I was going to tell, and they said they'd deny it, say they caught Molly doing it. And that . . ." He pauses and looks at Molly. "And that they had photos on a phone. Proof."

He shakes his head. "So I didn't know what to do. And then Coach came down on me really hard, saying I was messing with the team chemistry and we needed to put the team first."

I nod. "I get it. So you kept quiet."

Erik shakes his head. "No. I didn't." He looks slightly

sick. "I realized that I couldn't. It wasn't okay, you know? Like Derek's friends, in that story we read. They couldn't keep supporting him when he did that stuff. So I told Ms. Lewiston everything"—he looks over at her, and she smiles a little—"yesterday. But then the cameras were ruined, and you freaked out, and everything blew up."

"You told?" I ask. I look at him, then at Ms. Lewiston.

She nods. "He did. We were in the process of discussing how best to get to the truth of the issue in the way that caused the least harm." She glances at Molly. "Erik was in a tough position. But I have to say"—she smiles at him—"I'm very proud and impressed that you came forward."

Erik's face is blotchy, like he might cry.

I think about all he's risking to speak the truth. "That's . . . ," I start, but I don't know what to say. I want to apologize for suspecting him, for assuming I knew him. For assuming the worst. A hot ball of shame sits in my chest. Am I as judgmental and closed-minded as I think everyone else is?

I try to talk. "Yesterday, what I said . . . I never should have said that. I didn't mean it, okay? I—"

Erik cuts me off. "We're cool, Theo. Sometimes you just lose it and wind up fouling someone who really doesn't deserve it. I get it."

I actually *don't* get what he's talking about, but I nod anyway. "Thanks, but seriously. What I said to you"—I look around—"to all of you. It's not just that I shouldn't have said it. It wasn't what I think of you. I'm sorry."

"It's all good," Andre says. "It was a rough day. I get it."

"It's all good!" Alice echoes.

Molly nods.

I smile, feeling so relieved that my face almost does the chipmunk thing. "Thanks," I say finally. I put out my hand toward Erik. "For telling, I mean. Thank you."

He reaches across the table and shakes my hand, his massive and hot and calloused. "You're welcome," he says. "I should have . . . I should have realized sooner that they're . . . you know. But they're not always like that. I mean, I guess sometimes they are, but . . . for Kevin, things have been really bad at home for a while. His older brother started using drugs and got kicked off the high school team, and his parents pretty much freaked. And Shaun only made the team this year, and he used to be a really chill guy. I think he's trying to fit in." He sighs. "I guess that doesn't matter. They shouldn't have done it. Real talk? I thought your photos were sick. I really liked them."

Molly nods, her face still small and pale. "They were really amazing, Theo. My . . . Before my brother died, my parents had a photographer take photos of us, and we look stiff and stupid. I wish you had done them. Yours were . . . They looked so . . . true. You know?"

A small flare of heat hits my cheeks, and I try not to chipmunk-smile. "Really? I mean, thanks."

We all shuffle in our seats after that, and it's a little awkward. But then Alice says, in her bright-chirp voice, "So Blaine and Kevin and those guys drew all over them the first time, and Mr. Saunders's son threw out the cameras the last time. But who ruined them in the darkroom?"

And once again, the stomach-clenching feeling comes back.

CHAPTER 29

Sometimes I Laugh Hysterically Like a Weirdo in the Face of Truth and Justice

Everyone looks around the room again, side-eyeing each other. Well, everyone except Alice, who once again is more focused on getting the blood to drip down from her new wound. And Jax, who . . .

Jax, who is looking down at his clenched fists, like he wants to disappear.

Oh.

Eventually all of our eyes land on him. He doesn't look up at first, and I get even more of the hot, sweaty feeling. I *like* Jax. I like his sense of humor, and how he rolls his eyes over his dads' sea shanties (sea shanties! Seriously!) but was all worried about getting his younger brother's Matchbox cars back to him. I like how he got us all playing yoga-ball soccer but then made sure everyone had fun, like he was hosting a party or something. I don't want to think about him ruining my stuff.

"Jax . . . ," I start.

"It was an accident." His voice is so quiet I can barely hear.

"What?"

"When I opened the darkroom door. It was an accident. I had forgotten my planner in there, and I've lost, like, three planners already this year, and everyone from my dads to Davis to the school shrink keeps lecturing me, and so I turned back and ran down the hallway to get it before the next bell. I didn't even look at the sign on the door, Theo. I swear." He falls silent for a second, then gives a mean-sounding, not-funny laugh. "I'm a total screwup and I suck at life, but I didn't mean it."

We're all quiet after that. Everyone looks at me, and for a second I wonder why; then I realize. They're waiting for me to respond. To tell him I'm mad, or forgive him, or whatever.

I burst out laughing.

Alice, who's still watching me like I'm a zombie movie she can't wait to see the end of, squeaks, then laughs too, a high-pitched *tee-hee-hee*.

That does it. Serious, tears-streaming-down-my-face, stomach-hurts belly laughs erupt, and I can't help it.

"Dude?" Jax asks, his voice worried. *"DUDE?"*

And that makes me laugh harder. I slap at the table, barely able to breathe. Somewhere in the back of my mind I realize I'm falling off the edge of hysteria.

Erik starts laughing too, either at me, losing it completely, or at Alice, who's now silently rocking back and forth, wheezing.

"Sorry! Sorry, sorry, sorry," I say, gasping. "I just . . . You can't imagine how it's been, thinking that someone really hates me, hates me so much that they would follow me around, ruining everything I made. I mean, yes, I kept saying it was my photos, but it felt like *me*, like I had a target on my back and somewhere someone was taking aim, again and again. I had this whole conspiracy thing going in my mind, that someone had so much horrible energy to devote to my misery. And it turns out . . ." Laughter bubbles up again, and I have to lay my head on the table for a second.

"SORRY! I just . . . Freaking Jude, Shaun, Blaine, and Kevin, who, sorry, Erik, are pretty much total walking dumpster fires to everyone. And then Jax, who just needed his planner, and then Mr. Saunders's kid . . . There was no evil plan!"

I lean back in my seat, exhausted but feeling so, so light. I look at Jax, who seems somewhere between amused and concerned.

"Jax. Dude. Seriously, believe me when I say, it's all right. I mean, yeah, I was bummed about those prints. But—" I hesitate, then push on. Everyone else here has been honest; now it's my turn.

"But here's the thing. It was never really about the photos. I can always take more. I'm just really glad no one hates me." I start giggling again.

Jax joins in, shaking his head. "Jeeeeeez. If I had known how happy it'd make you, I could have saved it for your birthday or something."

I try to stop laughing. It's not *that* funny, obviously. But I guess I hadn't realized how much this nameless, faceless enemy had gotten in my head. It *had* felt personal, like some unknown hater was dogging me, waiting for me to expose myself, be vulnerable in any way, to humiliate me again.

Jax and Erik are talking about how hard it is to keep track of the school planners, and Alice is speaking quietly to Molly, whose eyes are red but who seems calmer now. And I know Alice is probably talking about zombies or flesh wounds or how to realistically gouge out an eye, but whatever it is, Molly seems totally into it.

Andre turns to me. His face is undecided for a minute, then he half shrugs and starts to speak.

"I know what you mean, by the way. I work really hard

to stay under the radar here. It's not worth it to me—I got my band and friends from church and, you know, a life. But that's all outside. And in here I'm, like, invisible. Which is fine—I want it that way. Means no one's messing with me or looking to make trouble. But when no one even noticed I wasn't there . . . well. It felt like maybe it wasn't so cool to be invisible, you know?"

I glance at him. As always, he's wearing dark jeans and some kind of not-stylin'-but-not-aggressively-nerdy sweater. It's easy to miss if you're not looking closely, but when I really look, I see he also has some fabric and leather bracelets, and his geek glasses are actually kind of hipster.

Ms. Lewiston clears her throat, and the talk dies down. She looks around.

"So. Let me start by saying, Jax, that I really appreciate your honesty. It's hard to speak up, and I recognize that this was really difficult for you."

She looks at him and smiles, and Jax grins back, his relief showing in his tipped-back chair and jiggling leg. "Before we finish up, though, can you talk a bit about why you didn't let Theo know? I realize it was an accident, but even so. His work was damaged for the second time, after a very serious and public vandalism incident, and it was your unintentional action that caused it. And it really upset him, because he thought he was being targeted in a sustained way. Did you think about telling him?"

Jax drops his chair to all four legs and folds back up. He looks at me, then looks away.

I want to tell him it's all good, but part of me wants to know too. I mean, Mr. Smith wasn't about to go raging over an accident, even if it did mess stuff up.

"Jax?" Ms. Lewiston says again, quietly.

Jax sighs. "I'm just . . . tired of messing up, you know?" His voice is low, and I lean forward to hear him. "I know it was an accident, and Smitty wasn't going to freak, but still. I figured there was a good chance I'd get blamed, or at least be under major suspicion for what happened in the gallery. And it'd be all about Jax the Screwup again. Another conversation with a teacher who's all 'I'm so disappointed, Jax.' Or 'You're going to need to try harder, Jax.' Or, my favorite, 'We're going to have another talk with your parents, Jax.'" He shakes his head, and his eyes are shiny bright, but he blinks fast and pulls his hat down. "It's my bad, for sure. I never thought it would turn into this whole thing with vacation week and Justice Circle and stuff. I didn't want to deal with it, and figured since the prints were ruined, there wasn't much point in talking about it."

"Like the neighbor's window," Alice says.

We all spin to look at her. I gasp. "Jeez, Alice!" I blurt before I can stop myself.

She grins. There are now maggots coming out of the new gash on her cheek.

Ms. Lewiston, with what looks like serious effort, pulls her eyes from Alice. "You make a really good connection, Alice. This is what we talked about in the library. What's the point of telling the truth if the damage is already done? The photos were ruined, no matter what. But, Jax, like your neighbor, Theo was left worried that someone had it in for him. Which is a very different feeling from knowing someone made a mistake. Do you understand the difference?"

Jax nods. "Yeah." He pauses, then says, almost like he's annoyed, "And I told my neighbor two days ago about his window. He freaked out, big-time, but we're cool now."

Ms. Lewiston smiles. "Jax, that's fantastic. I'm really glad to hear it." She leans down and rustles around in her bag. "Here. You earned it." With that she arcs a handful of Starburst across the table.

Not surprisingly, Molly shrieks and reaches for them. Mayhem ensues, of course, with Jax, Molly, and Erik nearly killing each other for the red Starburst while

Andre, Alice, and I watch. I catch Ms. Lewiston's eye, and she smiles.

"Pssst. Theo." She slides something across the table at me. It's a caramel bull's-eye.

I laugh, even though part of me feels shaky. I wanted to know. And now I do. But something still feels unfinished.

CHAPTER 30

Day Five Assessments

Date: Feb. 22

Name: *Molly Claremont*

What happened and what were you thinking at the time of the incident?

Well, it's kind of a long story. Or maybe it's not.

A group of boys—Kevin Hellson, Blaine Travis, Jude Moore, Shaun Wender—vandalized Theo's photographs. I walked in and saw them doing it, but they just laughed and handed me a marker, and I didn't want them to get mad; I wanted them to leave.

I drew on one of the photos.

Then they ran away, and I stayed there. And didn't tell anyone.

What have you thought about since?
There hasn't been a minute since it happened that I haven't wished I had done things differently. That I haven't wished I had never picked up the marker, that I had yelled right away.

But also . . . this whole week I've thought about Theo's photographs, which are amazing, and how much they mean to him. I don't love anything like he loves photography. I hadn't really thought about it before. It must be nice, to care about something like that.

What about this has been hardest for you?
Lying. Lying again and again, right to Theo's face.

What do you think needs to be done to make things as right as possible?
I apologized, and Jax apologized, and Mr. Saunders's son obviously didn't have any idea what he was doing. As for Blaine and Kevin and Shaun and Jude . . . I have no idea. I mean, maybe if they did a Justice Circle and really "processed" it with Ms. Lewiston and Theo, they'd get somewhere. But if I'm honest . . . I doubt it. I guess that's pretty unfair, though. They probably have their own stories.

Is there anything at all you'd like to share confidentially with Ms. Lewiston?

Just that I'm so sorry. I don't even know who I am anymore.

Name: Andre Hall

What happened and what were you thinking at the time of the incident?

Like I said, I wasn't even in the gallery, just my bag was. But I'll tell you, this whole week has made me wonder if being invisible is such a good plan.

What have you thought about since?

I've been thinking a lot about Theo being brave enough to put the photos up, and how it would feel to let people at school know about my music. I don't know. It could be cool. Scary, but cool.

What about this has been hardest for you?

Thinking Theo was getting messed with was scary, because it reminded me how easy it would be for me to be a target. I don't like that feeling.

What do you think needs to be done to make things as right as possible?

Theo needs to take more photos. They need to go back up on that wall.

Is there anything at all you'd like to share confidentially with Ms. Lewiston?

If I'm being honest, I'm kind of glad Alice never spoke up about my not being there, because it meant I spent the week here with these guys. And this week...I think it's changed us. I don't know exactly how, but things feel different now.

Name: *Erik Estrale*

What happened and what were you thinking at the time of the incident?

This whole thing has been like a nail-biter playoff game . . . no idea who's coming out on top, and the stakes are HUGE. This was the toughest game of my life, that's for sure. It was the worst, sitting in the locker room and listening to the guys laughing, and slowly figuring out what they were cracking up about. What kind of person loves trashing someone else's work? I hate—HATE—having to rat out my team. And I know they're not bad guys. I get that Theo thinks they are. But I know them, and they can be really funny, and loyal to the team. But I can't be down with what they did. I won't do that. Even knowing what's going on with Kevin and his parents, or that Shaun's worried that he's not really one of the team yet . . . that doesn't really matter, you know? Once I knew they did it, I couldn't un-know it.

What have you thought about since?
I've had to think A LOT this week. About how Alice and the other people in this Justice Circle are a lot more interesting than I knew. Even though I feel pretty bad about my friends—or, I guess I should call them my former friends—acting this way, I'm glad I got to know these guys a little bit. Like, maybe just because someone's my teammate doesn't mean they have to be my friend. And just because someone isn't on my team doesn't mean we can't hang out.

What about this has been hardest for you?
Realizing that my friends would do something like that to Theo . . . that's been pretty hard. You know

that expression "You look like you lost your best friend"? I feel kind of like that.

Also, if I'm being honest, I was really bummed to miss the basketball clinic, and I know Coach is still pissed. I'll be running wind sprints until I puke, and that's a fact. But I guess it's all worth it.

What do you think needs to be done to make things as right as possible?
As soon as I told about what I heard, it felt like I put down a 130-pound bench-press weight. And we all know how good that feels. I feel pretty awesome, all things considered. Yesterday was downright brutal, because I told the truth, and then the cameras were trashed, and Theo freaked out, and I thought we were all going to be suspended anyway. I thought it was all over. Now Theo's laughing and Jax is eating Starburst, and everyone's smiling. It's kind of like one of those Cinderella-story come-from-behind victories. And I love those.

Is there anything at all you'd like to share confidentially with Ms. Lewiston?
Just . . . maybe talk to Kevin and those guys. They're not all bad, I promise.

Name: Alice Shu

What happened and what were you thinking at the time of the incident?

It's strange, answering this question again and again. At the time of the incident...I was thinking the same thing I said the first day. But if you ask what I've been thinking SINCE...that's a different question. Here's what I think:

- Theo made assumptions about all of us, and about the school. He looked at the evidence and came up with a logical hypothesis: someone hated him and wanted to mess with him.
- That hypothesis was based on faulty evidence. In a movie, the director makes things happen to present information in a certain light without giving everything away. So the main character sees things but doesn't always know what they mean.
- This Justice Circle was a good idea, though it didn't always seem like it.
- I need to be braver about speaking up. I should have spoken up.

What have you thought about since?

A series of unrelated decisions—some malicious and some honest mistakes—brought us here. Now that we're here and the truth is out, what happens next is up to us.

What about this has been hardest for you?

Nothing, really! I had a pretty fun week. I wonder if these people will still be nice to me on Monday?

What do you think needs to be done to make things as right as possible?

I doubt anyone else would want to do it, but I kind of want to keep this group together.

Is there anything at all you'd like to share confidentially with Ms. Lewiston?

I wish

   I need

   I would like it if people like Kevin and Blaine would leave me alone. I would like it if people like Jax and Molly and Erik and Andre and Theo would <u>not</u> leave me alone. I'm not sure how to make that happen.

Name: Jax Fletcher

What happened and what were you thinking at the time of the incident?

So now it's out there. I forgot my planner, I was late, I ran right into the darkroom without looking. I completely screwed up, and the funny thing is, I didn't even know I had done anything wrong until the next day, when Smitty told everyone. My first thought was all "Oh man, poor Theo. That sucks that someone messed up his stuff again, after that disaster in the gallery. But it wasn't me." And it wasn't until later that I was like "AW NO! THAT <u>WAS</u> ME!"

Anyway, I should have told. Obviously I should have told.

What have you thought about since?

I've been freaking out all week, because I hate lying. But I REALLY didn't want to get blamed for the graffiti and everything, and it didn't seem worth it to speak up. But the thing is, the more you don't tell, the more you CAN'T tell. It felt like if I told on Day One everyone'd be super mad that they had to come in for my screwup. And then by Day Four I...I didn't want to tell Theo.

What about this has been hardest for you?

This kept growing into a bigger and bigger deal. And truth? It's been stressing me out something serious. Like, not sleeping well, feeling bad and everything. And the more I hung with Theo, the worse it felt.

What do you think needs to be done to make things as right as possible?

I was trying to make things as cool as I could here this week. Trying to make people laugh, trying to get Theo to make those new pinhole cameras. I guess I hoped I could make up for ruining his stuff without ever telling anyone. But it doesn't work that way.

Is there anything at all you'd like to share confidentially with Ms. Lewiston?

That restorative justice stuff? That was seriously dope. I might want to learn how to run groups like that when I grow up. If I can get through middle school first.

Name: Theo Gustav

What happened and what were you thinking at the time of the incident?

I thought I knew what happened, even though I didn't want to admit it to myself. I thought someone hated me, that someone in this school was targeting me again and again, and that everyone else either agreed that I was worth targeting, or just didn't care, or wanted to laugh at me. I thought it was only going to get worse, and more humiliating, and I didn't think anything that happened this week would make it better.

Turns out I was wrong about everything.

What have you thought about since?

I guess I've thought about the way we think about ourselves, and about everyone else. I was the victim, obviously, but after a few days I realized that I couldn't really hold on to that feeling of being totally right. The fact is, I was judging my classmates just as much—maybe more—than they were judging me. And maybe we're all the victims, and the ... you know, perpetrators. Maybe.

What about this has been hardest for you?

I really really really didn't want to think about how awful it felt to be the target of all this hate. I kept pretending it was only about my photos, and whoever did it has no artistic judgment. But it wasn't just the photos. It was ME.

What do you think needs to be done to make things as right as possible?

Here's the thing. I want people to know that Kevin and those guys did it, but I don't want Molly to get in trouble. I realize that's maybe unfair, but whatever. If it were up to me, that's what I'd want.

The only thing that still kind of bugs me? I still feel like sharing my photographs is a bad idea. And I hate that. I don't want to feel that way. I don't know . . . I think maybe I'm not as brave as I thought I was.

Is there anything at all you'd like to share confidentially with Ms. Lewiston?

What's weird is that in a way I think I was using the fact that this bad thing happened to make me bulletproof—thinking, "Hey, I've been wronged, I'm the victim here, so everyone owes me." But . . . there were other victims too. And . . . I'm not saying this is at all my fault, but the truth is I've stood by plenty of times while other stuff has gone down at school. I get why people kept quiet.

I guess I never really thought about it, but everyone can be the victim, the bystander, or even the perpetrator, depending on the day.

Also, I guess I want to say thank you. I couldn't have imagined the week would end this way.

suspicions or confused of it in her case they're the sam...

CHAPTER 31

Mr. Saunders Deserves Some Kind of Special Prize for His Efforts in Davis-Thwarting, but We Still Need Justice, Whatever That Looks Like

We're all scribbling away when the outer office door bangs. Alice squeaks and shoves her paper under her butt. The rest of us finish writing as Ms. Davis charges into the room. She has a streak of dust along the side of her black blazer and what looks like a cobweb on top of her head. I stare down at the conference table so I don't laugh.

"I hope and assume you've maintained the detention rule of silence?" she asks, looking around. "I apologize, children, that I can't remain in here today to finish this detention week *appropriately.*" She glares at Ms. Lewiston, who glares right back.

Alice is now gazing right at the cobweb, her mouth open.

I cough. "Um, Ms. Davis—"

Her eyes land on me and narrow. I can't decide if she's

suspicious or confused or if in her case they're the same thing.

"Mr. Gustav. May I ask why you've decided to return? You are excused from this detention. As the victim, you are not required to be here."

Man, she really loves the word *detention*. It's like each time she says it, she's really saying "chocolate" or "raspberries." The woman has serious issues.

I cough again. "I know. But the process we went through with Ms. Lewiston for the Justice Circle was really useful, and I kind of wanted to come back and finish it."

Ms. Lewiston opens her mouth like she wants to say something, but the walkie-talkie screeches and we all cringe.

"Of all days!" Ms. Davis mutters, and reaches for it. "Yes? What is it, Roy? Over."

We can all hear Mr. Saunders's voice crackling through the walkie-talkie. "Ms. Davis, ma'am, I'm still down here in the storage room. I know you said to try stacking all the liquids on the far wall, but unfortunately when I was moving them, the file cabinet with all your old files tipped over, and now I'm trying to sort them back out. But your filing system's a little confusing, so—"

Ms. Davis looks livid. Between the cobweb and her

squinty eyes, she could be in one of Alice's horror films. "Roy! My filing system was very specific. Please leave it. I'll be right down. Over."

We all stare in silence at the table, except Jax, who has his chin in his hands and is watching Davis like she's the best YouTube video ever. She scowls at him and scratches at her neck, recoiling at the dust that comes off.

"I am needed elsewhere," she says, and I silently send prayers of gratitude to Mr. Saunders.

She turns to me. "As I was saying, as the victim, Theo, you don't need to be here. I can call your mother—"

"I'm not 'the victim,'" I interrupt. "Or at least, that's not all I am. That's not the whole story. We've discussed it, and—"

But before I say any more, the walkie-talkie screeches again, and Davis gives a snort of annoyance. "Enough. I have to go, but rest assured that when I come back to dismiss everyone for the day, I will either have answers as to who the perpetrator is or I will be suspending *all* of you."

She looks at me again, and her lips thin. "And while you have chosen to be here, you will please respect the rules of silence as well."

With that, she sweeps out of the room in a move that would be dramatic if she didn't have a paper towel stuck to her shoe and another huge cobweb across her butt.

Once she's gone, everyone relaxes. Alice pulls her paper out from under her and hands it to Ms. Lewiston. Once Ms. Lewiston has collected them all, she reads through them, nodding as she reads.

When she's done, she looks up. "Okay. Here's the thing." She leans back and looks around. "I am so, so proud of you kids. This has been a hard week. Heck, this has been a hard year. Some of you are walking through fire right now, and you are doing it with grace and grit." Her eyes stray to Molly, and she gives a soft smile. "But let's do this. Let's stop fronting and be honest.

"Molly, love. You need to get some help. You can't keep this up, even if you are the most organized, hardworking seventh grader the world has ever seen. You cannot parent your parents while they mourn. It doesn't work that way."

Molly doesn't say anything, but nods, tears pooling in her eyes.

"So this group is going to help. Right?" she continues, looking around at us.

We all make *uh-huh* noises, except Alice, who cries, "Of course!"

"I'm going to talk to the school counselor about getting names of some therapists for your parents and for you. And what about you guys? How do you think you can help?"

We're all silent for a minute. I think about my mom,

whose default way of helping is to bring people books or meals. We could definitely bring some meals over to Molly's house, so at least she doesn't have to cook.

Jax speaks up. "I can be in charge of Operation Fun Times. You know, get something going, like . . . oh, I don't know. Off the top of my head . . . mayyyyyybe . . . yoga-ball *soccer*! Doesn't that sound fun?"

We all carefully look anywhere but at each other.

"That sounds . . . interesting. But whatever you want. Shenanigans. You're on it," Ms. Lewiston says, and Jax grins.

"I think I can manage that."

"And in exchange, because this is *quid pro quo* time, Molly, you're helping Jax get his school stuff organized. That does NOT mean"—she continues, because Jax appears to be dying by violent poisoning—"that does not mean color-coding his notebooks. That means checking in with him at the end of class and making sure he has the homework written down. That means texting after school or in the morning and making sure things like finished homework and his planner are coming back to school."

Molly straightens up and sniffles a little, but her voice is strong. "I can *totally* do that. I have a whole system of backpack checks and stuff. I check my sister's homework folder every night."

Jax rolls his eyes. "Are you sure this isn't my punishment?" he asks, but he shakes his head and grins. "That'd be cool, though. Seriously, I'll take any help I can get at this point. I just want everyone off my back."

Ms. Lewiston eyes him. "You have to be willing to actually *do* this, right, Jax? So if Molly texts and says 'Make sure your math assignment is in your folder,' you don't text back 'Sure!' and keep playing FIFA, right? You actually stand up and double-check that the sheet of paper is in your folder."

Jax laughs. "It's like you're living in my house, Ms. Lewiston. It's a little scary."

"I've seen it all before. You're not alone, my friend," Ms. Lewiston says. Then she turns and looks at the rest of us. "How else can you all help each other out?"

Jax leans forward. "Yo, Erik, you know the end-of-season team videos are always brutal. Totally boring, bad sound . . . a snoozefest. What if you work with our girl Alice—"

But we don't find out right away what Alice would do for Erik, because in a spectacular gesture of no-chill, Erik tips his chair over and falls off it with a crash.

Wow. The boy is a mess.

By the time he gets up and finishes apologizing (not sure for what, exactly, other than having no game), we've moved on. But eventually we agree that Erik will help Alice start videoing games and putting together end-of-season films for each team. Alice's eyes light up and she squeaks and doesn't even seem that disappointed when Ms. Lewiston warns her that the videos need to be realistic and uplifting, with no horror effects whatsoever.

And finally, Andre and I agree that I'll take head shots and live stills of Skeleton Curse. Because they have some big meetings coming up with potential agents (!!) and need professional but also seriously dope photos for the press kit.

When we're finished with all the deals and projects, Ms. Lewiston leans back and crosses her arms. "This is great. We're almost there. But there's still something we need to address."

We've all started talking over each other, making plans for photo shoots or basketball playoffs or a meet-up in Jax's backyard for yoga-ball ice hockey on his rink (I can't help thinking this is a potentially disastrous idea, but he swears that he has extra helmets). But eventually we all stop talking and look at Ms. Lewiston.

"Restorative justice requires that we close out by ensuring that you, Theo, have a sense that justice has been done. We've learned a lot, and we've become closer as a group, but let's go back to what happened, and how we as a community, regardless of our guilt or innocence, can make amends."

I lean forward. "Actually, I've been thinking about that, and I have an idea."

Everyone's looking at me now. Part of me wants to stick a sock in my own mouth so I'll stop talking, but I can't seem to make myself shut up, even though I'm breaking my own solemn lifetime vow of five days ago. Apparently I'm terrible at solemn lifetime vows.

"So here's the thing: Ms. Davis thinks she knows us. Heck, I thought I knew you guys, and I was totally wrong. And I don't know how she's going to find the 'perpetrator' unless we tell her how it all went down. Which honestly, I don't really want to do. I mean, Ms. Lewiston, you can tell her about Kevin and Blaine and those guys, but since we have no evidence . . ."

Ms. Lewiston nods. "Even without evidence, I can bring them in and talk with them. Let me handle that part. And, Molly, I think your role has already been dealt with. Not to worry."

Molly nods, her eyes still red.

Jax opens his mouth, then closes it again. Finally he says, "I'll tell her. I mean, that I screwed up with the darkroom. And maybe you can say about Teddy John—"

"I got the feeling maybe Mr. Saunders didn't want to make that a big deal," I say, thinking about his face as we talked about his son coming to work with him.

Jax grunts. "Yeah, knowing Davis, bringing his kid to work would be a serious infraction. She'd get poor old Saunders in detention if she could."

I nod. "Exactly." Taking a deep breath, I go on. "Look. I just thought . . . what if I hang a new show? A series of photos? Of you. Of us. Trying to . . . you know . . ." I trail off, and I get the sweaty-embarrassed feeling again. "You know, trying to show our real selves. Or something."

My face is probably approaching Molly levels of red, and I shake my hair down in front of me. The memory of the gallery show is neon bright, and so is the mosquito buzz of the whispers and giggles and gossip when the show got vandalized. It makes my stomach cramp, honestly. I swore I wouldn't do this again. Why would I do this again?

I remember why. Because, not to be pathetically earnest, but . . . that's not who I want to be. I clear my throat. "And that would be our . . . like, closure. We'd tell Davis that this was the 'justice' we agreed to." I pause. "I mean, you don't have to. Obviously. It might be a really bad idea."

Silence.

I'm tempted to keep talking, to tell them I'm kidding or ask Ms. Lewiston what she thinks. But I remember my mom telling me that sometimes the most powerful way to say something is to hold your words and let other people fill the silence. So I wait.

"I'm in," Andre says suddenly, and his voice is loud. "I think your photos are dope, and I don't know what the point is of staying so quiet. What the heck? Take a photo of me drumming, or on a yoga ball, or whatever. Let's do it."

My face-spreading chipmunk smile is unstoppable. "Yeah? That's . . . that's sick. Thanks."

"I'm in too," Molly says. "What's the worst that will happen? People will make fun of me? Please." Her voice turns steely. "Compared with everything else right now, that's like . . ." She waves a hand like she's shooing away a fly. "What. Ever." She's got the full-on Everything Is Disgusting voice going, but this time it cracks me up.

"You can definitely take my photo!" Alice chirps. "I think that would be awesome! Let me see if I can add an eyeball really quick."

"Yeah, I'm in," Jax says. "Your photos *are* sick, Theo."

"Me too," Erik says. "Just . . . can you not make me look too dumb?" He blushes.

I nod. "I will make you look awesome," I promise. "I'll make you look *real*."

CHAPTER 32

The Justice Club Gets Its Photo Shoot, and It Is Legit Awesome

We have to move fast. Ms. Lewiston promises to be our lookout, so we tiptoe through the office and into the front hall, where the afternoon sunlight is streaming in. Even though it's barely three o'clock, the sun is low and orange.

It's perfect.

I move each of them around, first positioning everyone by themselves against the sunlit wall. There's a mad dash to the gym for a basketball, which photographs as a blur of movement in Erik's hands. And Andre pulls drumsticks out of his bag, so we quickly improvise a few stools and empty file boxes, and he whales away on them. I snap one of Molly jumping, an explosion of energy, and another of her looking past me, her face shadowed and mysterious. One by one I try to capture them, making them laugh, waiting until they think I'm not watching, circling behind them so that I get just a slice of a face, lit with the blazing sun.

Then it's time for the group shot. I drag a chair out of the nearest classroom, prop the camera on it, and fiddle with the exposure, making sure everyone is in the frame. The five of them are sitting in a row on the banister (rule infraction, of course, but artists have to break the rules). There's room for me in the center, and the shadows from the slanting sun make them look mysterious and larger-than-life. The only problem is that, even with a textbook yanked from the lost and found, I can't get the camera to stay put.

Suddenly there's a faint whistle. Alice squeaks and almost falls off the banister. Davis must be on the move. Whipping up my shirt, I yank my belt off my pants.

Jax calls out, "Go, sexy!" but I ignore him and try to strap the camera in place.

"There! Quick, make room!" I say, sprinting toward them. I push myself up on the banister and let my hair fall forward right as the camera clicks.

"Okay, I'll check it later. Let's go!" I grab my belt but abandon the chair and the book, and we race back to the office.

Ms. Lewiston's standing in the doorway, looking a little stressed. "I told her you were all on bathroom break. That I sent you all at once so you didn't keep disrupting the group at different times! Quick!"

We slide into our seats, red-faced and a little sweaty, but in place. Within seconds Davis walks in. I try not to gasp. Her shoes are making a weird squelching noise, and there are now so many cobwebs in her hair that she looks like she's gone gray.

Her eyes narrow. "There's a chair in the hallway. Why is there a chair in the hallway?"

We all stare at the table. Predictably, Alice squeaks a little bit.

"Well?"

Erik looks up, his face a model of respect. "Could you describe the chair, ma'am?" he asks.

"It's a chair! A regular classroom chair! What is it doing in the hallway?" Davis says.

Andre looks up. "Why would we move a chair to the hallway?" he asks, as polite as can be.

"That's what I'm asking you!" Davis yells.

Alice squeaks again.

Molly raises her hand. "Maybe it was a poltergeist. I heard there was an ancient burial ground for condemned witches in our town."

Ms. Davis looks like she might actually swing at something.

"There is. No. Poltergeist." She looks around. "Really? No one will admit to this?"

"To what?" Jax asks. "The world is a mysterious place. A chair in the hallway is hardly the greatest mystery of them all."

"It's true!" Alice adds. "For instance, there are these totally creepy giant crop circles that just showed up in New Zealand, and no one knows why. That's a true mystery!"

I keep staring at the table, suddenly realizing the camera bag is sticking out by my feet. I send up a silent prayer that Davis won't walk over.

She looks around at us, but everyone is poker-faced. Ms. Lewiston is looking calmly right at Davis.

Finally Davis slams her hands, which are almost black with dust, down on the table.

"Okay. Fine. You have another hour—" Before she can go on, her walkie-talkie gives a screech.

"Ms. Davis? You copy? Over," comes Mr. Saunders's voice. I am going to owe that man the biggest Dunkin' Donuts coffee in the world.

Ms. Davis closes her eyes for several seconds, saying nothing, then opens them. "I will see you at dismissal," she announces. "To mete out your final punishment." And she spins on her heel (*squiiiiish!*) and leaves.

We all stay silent for a minute, in case she comes back. Then we collapse.

"OMG OMG OMG THAT WAS SO CLOSE!" Molly whisper-shouts.

Jax shakes his head. "We are seriously lacking in chill here, people. Come on."

I start to laugh. "Poltergeist?" I ask Molly. "Really?"

She turns her trademark Starburst cherry color and half smiles.

"It was the best I could come up with," she says, and Jax shakes his head.

"Rookie."

"Crop circles!" Andre adds.

It takes a while for the laughter to die down.

"Okay," I say finally. "Let's see what I got here."

I pull up the camera and start to look through the images. They're better than I hoped—stark and dramatic and *so* not-typical middle school shots.

I look up. "These are going to be awesome. If I rush and beg and call in a bunch of favors, I think I can get large-format prints done and have them framed for the student gallery this weekend." I stare at the photos on the tiny screen. "But right now, I really want to get one printed from the computer and leave it for Ms. Davis. You know, to say we've completed our 'process' and justice has been served."

I look at Ms. Lewiston. "If you'll help us, of course."

She nods. "Theo, that's all I've been trying to do."

CHAPTER 33

I Doubt Ms. Davis Will Like It, but This Is the Ending

So that's what we do. Ms. Lewiston fires up one of the office computers, and I use my memory card to pull off the best group shot. When I print it out, everyone crowds around me, and we all get quiet and awkward-happy-proud-weird all at once.

It's a great shot. We've all literally borrowed each other's hats, so Alice is wearing my fedora and Erik is wearing Jax's flat brim and Andre is wearing Molly's wool ski hat with the big pom-pom. Our arms are around each other. Some of us are looking up, and some of us are looking sideways at each other. Jax has his head thrown back, laughing. The slanting light puts us all in such deep shadow that it's not immediately clear who's who. All it looks like, at first glance, is a photo of six friends.

I look around. "So . . . what do you think?"

Molly has gone Starburst cherry–colored again, but she's smiling. "I think it's awesome. I mean, as a photograph. You're really talented, Theo. Seriously."

I try to keep my chipmunk smile back, but it's hard. "Thanks," I say. "But I meant, what do you think we should do? Just leave it for Davis?"

"Ms. Davis," Ms. Lewiston corrects me. "And if you're hoping to use this as closure, you'll need to say something more." She looks around. "You've done incredibly well with this process, all of you. And I think"—she glances at the clock, then back at us—"I think you should finish it on your own. In your own words." Picking up her bag and coat, she starts toward the door. "Dismissal is in ten minutes. I'm going to head out to talk with Ms. Davis before the end of the day. Once you finish here, you may wait outside for your parents." She smiles at us. "You've made me very proud," she says, and walks out of the room.

We look at each other.

"What are we supposed to do?" Jax asks. "Am I supposed to confess about the darkroom? Because I will, but—"

"No," I say, and my voice is louder than I meant it to be. "No, I don't want you to. Let's . . . let's leave her a note. And then let's get out of here."

Everyone nods and mutters, and I pull out a piece of paper.

Before I start writing, Alice raises her hand.

Molly has her Why Is Everyone So Stupid face on, but she says, fairly nicely, "Alice, you can just say something. You don't have to raise your hand."

Alice squeaks. "Oh! Well, I was wondering. Monday, at school . . ."

There's a pause.

Molly says, "I'll be texting Jax about his backpack and stuff. And maybe you and Erik can meet up before first bell and figure out what you're going to do for the basketball video."

Erik, who has been leaning on his elbow with his chin in his hand, promptly manages to punch himself in the face.

Jax closes his eyes as though he's in pain. "Dude," he mutters. He claps his hands together. "Yo, Alice, we're all going to be cool on Monday. Right? We're cool? We're, like, a band of brothers or something. Like grizzled old war veterans, you know?"

And it is a sign of how far we've come that we all nod in agreement like this makes sense.

Seven minutes later we leave our note and the photo faceup on the table and head out. As always, Molly's in front, storming through the doors like the boss of Bossville, but this time she waits and holds the door for the rest of us. Meanwhile, Alice holds on to Erik's arm as she tries to walk out backward, just to see if she can, while Andre and Jax move even slower, talking bands and shouting over each other.

And me? I'm laughing with Alice, waiting for the music nerds, but also watching, watching us, taking a picture in my mind of the six of us, walking out together into the late-winter sun.

EPILOGUE

Dear Ms. Davis,

*We wanted you to know that we finished our
Justice Circle, and justice has been served.*

*But let's be honest. You weren't really that
excited about this in the first place. As far as
you're concerned, we all had our roles: victims and
perpetrators, bullies and targets.*

*We're pretty sure you think you know
everything about us. You know us as the
Overachiever, the Jock, the Nerd, the Screwup,
the Weirdo, and, of course, the Victim. They're
the simplest definitions, a way of filling in the
whole picture from one small fragment. We all do*

it, all the time. Those labels fit, and we admit we thought they described us pretty well.

But we were wrong.

Because, as this photo shows, that fragment isn't close to the whole picture. Each one of us is more than our definition, and less obvious than you might think. Look at this photo, and ask yourself: How well do you know us after all?

In closing, we respectfully inform you that this Justice Circle worked. We got to the truth, and learned that the truth isn't as simple as we thought. There's a lot more to each of us than meets the eye. We know you wondered if there was any point to this Justice Circle. Please look closely at this photo. Does it answer your question?

> *Sincerely,*
> *The Justice Club*

ACKNOWLEDGMENTS

I always start a book alone in my head and end it with a full team of people. I count on them for everything from not letting me set my first draft on fire to fixing my horrible (mis)use of commas and ellipses. Writing books is a team sport, for sure.

Huge thanks and awkwardly long hugs for the first responders: my longtime critique partners who are there every single step of the process from "hey, I think I have an idea" to "OMG my author copies have arrived!" These patient and incredibly talented women read early drafts, help mull and brainstorm, talk me out of my tree when the writing is going badly, and celebrate all the milestones along the (very long) road from idea to book. Kate "Okay, But What If . . ." Boorman, Rachael "I FORGOT ABOUT SOCK PUPPETS" Allen, Alina "Read Me Bedtime Stories

Forever" Klein, and Jen "This Time We're Really Going to Write" Malone, I am so grateful. While we don't have a holiday cookie swap or a watercooler to hang around, having you as my virtual office mates makes everything better.

Next in line is the forever MVP Marietta Zacker and the rest of the Gallt & Zacker Literary team. Marietta, you are my sister from another mister, and I am so grateful for your guidance, wisdom, and friendship. And laughter. And teenager commiseration. Thank you for getting my sense of humor, for working to make books that will change the world, and for saying to me, gently and with great kindness, "Dude, sometimes you just have to write the book." Amen.

And of course I need a shout-out to the gang at Delacorte Press/Random House. Beverly Horowitz read a draft of what became my debut novel back in 2012 and has let me make up ridiculous stories ever since. Thanks to Krista Vitola, who bought *It Wasn't Me* when it was just a synopsis, and to Kelsey Horton, who took it from an idea to a finished book. And a special thanks to the copy editors, Colleen Fellingham, Alison Kolani, and Tricia Callahan, who dealt with my writing tics ("I mean," "I mean," "I mean") and made everything read better. Also big hugs to Bobby McKenna and Nicole Gastonguay, who created such a cool cover, and Josh Redlich and the publicity department, who help people know that I wrote a book.

And thanks of course to my family: Patrick, Noah, and Isabel. I write truer, braver, kinder, and better books because of you.

Finally, this book is dedicated to the educators—in my family, in my kids' classrooms, and around the country—for a reason. The teen and tween years are never easy, and middle school is, for many of us, a time when we commit to our definitions of ourselves as jocks, brains, or, most worryingly, screwups or good kids. I am so grateful for all of you who push our kids to look past those easy definitions, to question not only their classmates but themselves and what they are capable of. Thank you for doing the work.

AUTHOR'S NOTE

This book started with two very different idea sparks that have nothing to do with each other. First, there's the seriously awesome 1980s teen movie *The Breakfast Club*. If you haven't seen it, see it, because, like I said, it's seriously awesome and has probably the best quotes of any movie ever (with the possible exception of *The Princess Bride*). But second, there's a model of dealing with community conflict called restorative practice, or restorative justice, that keeps bubbling up in my life. And while *It Wasn't Me* isn't a book about restorative justice, the Justice Circle that Ms. Lewiston leads is very much influenced by it.

Most basically, restorative practice seeks to resolve conflicts or even proactively avoid conflicts by making sure everyone in a community is heard and valued. The goal is to repair the harm rather than just punish the person who inflicted it. This means that when a problem arises, instead of focusing on who's responsible and how to punish them, restorative justice seeks ways for the person who caused the harm to make amends so everyone involved can move forward.

Versions of restorative justice are used in schools, court systems, and all kinds of communities around the world. The model that is currently used in courts and schools started around forty years ago and is partially based on indigenous and tribal justice models that go back much farther but are also still widely used today in tribal nations across Canada and the United States.

So what does this all have to do with books for kids (or *The Breakfast Club*)? A lot, really. One of the biggest challenges for teens and tweens is the feeling of being judged, of being only whatever your teachers or classmates see on the outside. Whether they see a nerd or a jock, an overachiever or a weirdo, a screwup or a victim, doesn't matter. Whether we like the image we're showing the world or hate it really doesn't matter either. Because none of us is only one thing. All of us are more than meets the eye.

So for years, as I've watched my own kids' struggles in school, and watched incredible young friends battle to redefine themselves and grow, I've thought about how much we still need to learn. In schools, zero-tolerance models and harsh punishments often don't help an individual kid, or the rest of the community. Restorative justice isn't an easy answer, but it offers everyone, no matter how they see themselves or how other people see them, the chance to change their story.

If you're curious to learn more, there are great organizations that work in schools and communities. Just search the internet for *restorative justice in schools* to find case studies, training, and more. Some places to start include:

> centerforrestorativeprocess.com
> restorativejustice.org